MOSSBACK

By

Kenneth Fore

Second Edition

Copyright 2014

Copyright © 2014 Kenneth Fore
Library of Congress 2013902991
ISBN 978-0-9890320-2-5 EBook
ISBN 978-0-9890320-3-2

Dedicated

To Meghan, Samantha, and Sarah.

I'm not mad at deer like I use to be.

Chapter 1

In a dusk-dark swamp in South Alabama, Melvin waited for the buck. Not just any buck, but a world-record whitetail buck that had tormented him for four years now. The old man hunted only with his longbow and an Indian arrowhead he found several years back. He had attached the lethal arrowhead to a handmade arrow so when the time came, the arrow would fly true and deadly.

Some hunters and friends disagreed with him about the longbow, but he refused to carry any other weapon into the swamps. He told them, "The longbow's been used for thousands of years, and if it was good enough then, it's good enough now." But if he'd known what the next twenty-four hours held, he would have carried a cannon.

It was late November, the leaves were about gone, and it had rained off and on four days and nights straight. The outlines of ominous, dark purple clouds were building up, covering the horizon in the western sky. Not a good sign if you're in a freezing swamp.

Now it was almost dark, and a windblown rain had started to drizzle on him. He was cold, shivering; the time had arrived when he usually left the swamps and walked back to the camp house. He strained to see and listen, but the gusty wind pushed against the dark trees, and their naked limbs rolled and bounced. Across the bottoms, he saw winter-gray and black vines shake, disguising movements and baffling sounds. That didn't matter much, though. Like radar, Melvin could zero in on movements, could interpret the sounds made by the swamps. Even a bird's peep or a squirrel's yap had a specific meaning. He listened in and understood.

Melvin would have been out of place in any city, and he knew it. Those who didn't know him would doubt he could hold an intelligent conversation or understand things on a complex level. People who saw him for the first time might think he looked like a tall, unshaven outlaw, weary from a long cattle drive.

He carefully positioned the longbow on his lap, waiting and watching for the big buck to show. Moments later, he saw a fat doe cautiously easing along the bank of Narrow Gap Slough, a name he gave the slough years ago. There would be no celebration this evening. The doe passed him, unharmed.

Melvin remained optimistic. Forty-five days were left before deer season closed, but for Melvin, the constraints of time had no effect. He hunted the buck year-round in his mind, with thoughts and even rages about the buck's unnatural, near-banshee mystique.

He stood up slow and stretched out his arms from his six-one frame. In this stance, he inhaled the cool, damp air, taking in the odor of soggy swamp mud and decaying leaves, a scent to which he'd grown accustomed. In one smooth motion, he picked up the longbow and rested it on his right shoulder.

At sixty-seven, Melvin had the body of a well-conditioned man a dozen years younger, and his mind was sharp. At least, he hadn't noticed anything slipping, except that he remembered less about what happened yesterday. Others had seen the change in him, and a few made fun of him behind his back. He knew it and it hurt, because he knew in his heart they were right. Knew he shouldn't be hunting a mysterious ghost-buck at his age. Why should they believe him anyway? They hadn't seen it. No one else had spotted the big animal on Melvin's three-thousand-acre farm, only Melvin.

He scanned across the bottoms, and his washed-out green eyes drank in the crowds of strapping oak trees, cypresses, poplars, sweet gum trees and white oaks that stood strong and proud and dominated the bottoms.

He saw Narrow Gap Slough curl, then curve back against a beaver dam crammed full of red, gold, gray, yellow and brown leaves. The leaves floated on the surface of the gravy-colored water, and cypress knees rose like spikes three feet above it.

The raindrops multiplied, producing designs like shooting targets with rings that grew, then dwindled on the water's flat surface. He looked high into an oak tree and saw a cat squirrel steal an acorn before scooting out of sight.

After a few more minutes of careful observation, he started to walk in long strides, placing his rubber boots on the soaked leaves with care. Years of experience had taught him to move stealthily; instinct made him crouch and bend as he eased along.

He never got in a hurry—there was too much to see—and he never missed an opportunity to observe animals. Watching animals in their natural habitat was the highlight of most of his hunts. And, in over fifty years of deer hunting, he had occasionally bagged a big buck while walking out from a hunt. At least, until four years ago.

Melvin had opportunities to kill other bucks these past four winters, but he let them walk. He wanted one monster buck the one other hunters had named "the ghost-buck."

A nervous gray squirrel worked for acorns at the base of an oak tree, and Melvin stopped and watched. The squirrel didn't see him, and after a few moments, he started easing along the trail again.

He'd gone twenty yards when a screeching brown woodcock leapt up with pounding wings like a loud, beating roll on a bass drum.

Clenching his bow, he watched it climb like a wobbling football, until the plump bird arced into the air, then appeared to fall short of its intended landing.

A glance up at the clouds made Melvin decide to walk faster. If he couldn't see the stars, it would be easy to get turned around, prolonging his stay in the swamps. Becoming disoriented in the swamps with his knowledge about the monster buck and the storm's approach was more than he wanted to contend with.

Melvin didn't want to tangle with any animal in the dark, but he'd witnessed the buck's unnatural behavior over the course of several years, and always felt eyes staring at him, eyes pressing on his back when he eased out of the swamps in stumpy light. He knew the swamps well, but there was something about noises in a swamp in the dark that made the strongest man feel like a young boy. And, the rain had increased. As he picked up his pace he muttered, "Hope I can make it to the camp house before it pours."

The camp house was one of two dwellings on the farm, which had been in his wife's family for three generations. Both were over a hundred years old. The main farmhouse rested on the northwest section of the farm, a quarter mile from the camp house. Once an old shotgun house, Melvin had converted and remodeled it, over the course of several years, into a hunting cabin. It was a fitting use for it, he always thought with irony. A shotgun house derived its name because of its design—a person could shoot a shotgun through the front door and out the back and never hit a wall.

His friends and family who came to the farm to hunt or fish stayed at the camp house. Many times, they'd spend the night. Melvin preferred the camp house during hunting season, and now that he lived alone, he spent lots of his time there during the summer months, too.

The structure had gray tarpaper and shingles nailed horizontally on the exterior. The tarpaper was tacked into the wood and, over the years, many of the tacks had released rust-brown tears that stained the covering. River rocks from nearby Flat Creek supported the main beams of the dwelling, and two rock chimneys in need of repair stood on each side of the house. The dwelling had eight windows— two on each side. All were dark. Translucent plastic covered the windows, making them look eerie and cold.

Melvin made it off the choking path to the lane and headed toward the camp house. He stomped his boots against the ground several times to dislodge the clumps of sticky mud from them. The brim of his floppy camouflage hat kicked up, exposing his thinning gray hair.

As he walked, he looked up and saw the deeply bruised sky, felt the frigid cold in the gusts of wind, and knew he'd better hurry. Melvin was sure there'd be a soaking rain, or maybe ice, before too long.

A huge black walnut tree stood near the camp house. Grayish Spanish moss hung down from its bare limbs, looking like long, matted hair after a shower. The tree and moss moved in the breeze, and seemed to greet the old man as he walked up the path.

At the camp house, on the corner of the porch's cinnamon-colored tin roof, a piece of tin lifted, nearly folding, then fell, then rose and fell again with musical rhythm. He ignored it and walked up the steps onto the covered porch. Just then, rain fell angrily and the tin roof sizzled like bacon in a hot skillet.

The covered porch had a small addition for a bathroom.

The enclosed room had a commode; a freestanding sink that had once been white, with a mirror above it; and a tile shower installed ten years ago along with an electric water heater. A nearby well provided the water.

Melvin leaned the longbow up against the wall on the big porch—its tip nearly hit the ceiling—and went into the house, closed the door and flipped on the light switch. The door had never had a lock. Didn't need one. No stranger would casually venture onto the farm without him knowing about it. He did put value on the many photographs and other mementos in it, but nothing remained in the camp house worth stealing anyway.

He took a battered brown radio from a nearby chest-high shelf and shook it. All he got for his effort was a burst of static. That was just as well. The only time he listened to a radio was when Alabama played football.

The worn wood under the vinyl floor groaned when he walked across it to the four-burner stove. In the black cast-iron skillet rested a lake of ashen grease, with dark specks pushing up like tiny islands in a lifeless ocean. An ivory refrigerator was in one corner of the kitchen. The stove was in the opposite corner, and a space heater stood in between them, jutting toward the center of the large room. Both the stove and space heater used propane. Since power had been connected, the fireplaces weren't used.

From the ceiling's center, a single light bulb hung over the kitchen table from a braided brown electrical cord. The ceiling was heart pine tongue-and-groove stained gray, and the walls were constructed of heart pine and plaster. Solid and well built a hundred years before; Melvin saw no need to change them. On one wall were old photographs that filled him with memories: newspaper clippings of Coach Paul "Bear" Bryant and Alabama football.

To most standards, the camp house was luxuriously sized. Aside from the kitchen, there were six rooms. Those had old Army bunk beds for his friends and family, who used to hunt more than they did now.

He sat at the table on one of the two gray benches that stretched the length of it on each side and pulled off his rubber boots. Next, the damp camouflage coveralls, then his shirt and socks, which he hung on separate nails along the wall in his bedroom. There, he put on his camp house clothes: a wrinkled red and black wool shirt, baggy denim jeans, socks and worn-out deck shoes. He returned to the kitchen to prop his rubber boots upside down against the wall close to the heater.

Afterward, he walked to the sink, filled a kettle with water and placed it on the burner to heat. Only then did he go back through the door to the covered porch.

He put his right index finger into his mouth and wet it, then placed the finger above his head. The northwest side of the finger chilled. As he'd thought, the wind was growing strength out of the northwest, definitely not a good sign.

Looking through the trees, he saw lights bounce up, then down, and heard wheels spin and saw reflected taillights sway a couple of times as a vehicle lumbered up the winding lane. Between the trees and the falling darkness, he couldn't make out the vehicle.

"Who in the world is that coming in here in this kind of weather?" he muttered, and scrolled through a mental checklist of people who knew about the place. Barring an emergency, none of them would be willing to risk getting stuck in the mud-slick, potholed road to the camp house. He picked up his longbow and brought it inside, turned on the porch light and closed the door. By the time he heard the vehicle's door slam shut, he was at the kitchen table taking a slow drink of coffee.

Chapter 2

"YELP!" and then "Yoooo, Uncle Melvin!" came the cry from the person bouncing up the steps with a brown paper sack in his arms. Melvin smiled at the soft timbre that still managed to cut through the stillness.

"Alabama gonna beat Auburn tomorrow," Chad said happily, dropping the sack on the table at the same time his backside hit the bench across from Melvin. "Coach Bear Bryant has a *real* quarterback with Joe Namath. He's almost as good as Johnny Unitas and Bart Starr."

Melvin nodded. "The Bear don't lose much," he said, and grinned, remembering how he'd watched Chad mature from a five-year-old child to a full-grown man. Melvin's brother was a good father, but never hunted or fished, and he resented Chad spending so much time with his Uncle Melvin. But Melvin and Chad had formed a bond the minute Chad was old enough to take hunting with him, and Melvin's instincts about his nephew turned out right. When the time came, he essentially gave his business to Chad, and his nephew had diversified the grading and hauling business into a huge concrete, concrete block and pipeline company.

Chad didn't have it easy growing up. Not because he was poor. The ribbon factory didn't pay much, but his father managed to pay the bills. No, when Chad was eleven, he fell on a Popsicle stick. Caught him right in the throat. He also broke his nose and blackened his left eye: the first black eye he'd ever had. When Melvin rushed over to the house as soon as he heard what happened, he remembered that the color of the bruise matched Chad's light blue eyes.

Both injuries seemed to heal, but Chad's voice didn't sound right. The doctor concluded his voice box had been damaged. Now, years later, his baritone was soft. The damage prevented him from hollering or calling out at a high volume.

Melvin would have liked for Chad to play football at the University of Alabama. At six-one and two hundred and thirty pounds, Chad would have made a good guard—he was a smart offensive player, and a terror on defense. But when Chad sustained a concussion in his senior year in high school, the doctors wouldn't give him a waiver to play at the college level. He attended the University of Alabama anyway, and eventually graduated with a major in business. It took him five years—Chad had headaches that would come and go, but eventually, they stopped for good.

Chad was freethinking and willing to take calculated risks. Melvin had taught him to be frugal with his money, to be methodical and pay attention to details, so he was practical, just like his uncle. Even so, if Chad had been forced to work in a corporate environment, he wouldn't have made it. Melvin believed that kind of structured environment would break his spirit. So, when he was twelve, Melvin let him work with him in the grading and hauling business.

At first, Chad would do almost any task to earn pocket money. As he grew older, Melvin gave him more and more work to do. In the hot summer months as a teenager, and over summer breaks from college, he worked beside every man in the field. Because of the after-school and summer jobs, Chad had good work experience to bring to the business. The day he took it over, Melvin noted that Chad's lean face had lost its baby fat from hard work, and his narrow-bridged nose fit his face and made him ruggedly handsome.

Melvin held up his steaming cup. "How 'bout some coffee?"

"No thanks, Uncle Melvin. I can't stay long," Chad said, and grinned as he reached out, shoved the grocery bag aside and place his arm flat on the table, which was made of wood planks pulled together so tight the wood looked like it had grown together. On its surface was a variety of half-moon imprints, brown and black stains like brands long since fossilized, unable to be scrubbed out of the wood. "But I've gotta ask . . . Did ya see anything today?"

Melvin shook his head. "Floppy-ear doe is all."

Melvin had taught Chad how to hunt, fish, trap and survive in the swamps and forests. When Chad was younger, he was always excited about Fridays because he could go to the camp and hunt or fish the entire weekend with his uncle. During high school, he remained alone at the camp over the Christmas holidays and would hunt until he had to return to school the following week, with Christmas Day his only break. But after college, business and family took him away from what he loved. Nowadays, Chad hunted whenever he had the time.

Melvin rose from the bench and walked over to stand by the stove, sliding his hands into the rear pockets of his jeans. When he didn't speak, Chad continued.

"What a lousy drive in here! Man, I couldn't keep my truck tires from spinning in the mud. Bet I left fifty or more ruts all over Fannie Road." He shook his head and frowned. "Everything's a mess with this storm coming up. They say there's gonna be a lot of ice this time."

"It's a wonder you didn't get bogged down," Melvin said.

"I damn near did at that ole mud hole on the curve. We ought'a do something 'bout that." Chad looked up at the ceiling light and frowned, then returned his worried gaze to Melvin. "I saw some hail the size of dimes on the way here. Already there are a few tree branches down. It won't be long before a tree limb or tree falls on the power lines. Might be weeks before the power company can get round to making repairs."

"Could you tell how high the water is at Flat Creek?" Melvin asked ignoring Chad's implied question. Flat Creek branched off the Alabama River and traveled along the property line for over a mile. The creek was narrow in many places, but still wide and deep enough to travel with a small boat or canoe. Trees had fallen across it over the years, making it nearly impossible to travel without getting out and carrying your boat over a logjam. Melvin liked it that way, though. The abundant foliage, living and once alive, made game as abundant and diverse as sea life in the bottoms. However, the only way in and out of the property was the bridge over Flat Creek.

Chad leaned back and considered Melvin's question, his narrow brown eyebrows knitted in thought. "Well, when I went over the bridge, it looked 'bout ten feet, maybe higher. If it rains like they said, I'd say by morning the bridge might be several feet underwater. Flat Creek looks mighty angry."

"It's been angry before," Melvin said.

"The temperature's dropping fast, though. I listened to the weather on the way over. They're saying lots of high winds, large hail and heavy rains. And it's supposed to be at or near freezing for the next couple of days."

Melvin hadn't heard the forecast. Didn't have to. His wet finger and sore joints had told him the same thing Chad just did. Bad weather never bothered him, though. He believed even the worst weather could be a hunter's ally. The Flat Creek Bridge was another matter.

Chad sighed, and Melvin knew his nephew had decided to stop beating around the bush.

"I've been giving it a lot of thought, Uncle Melvin." Chad fixed his gaze on Melvin's eyes. "Why don't you call it quits and come home with me? I'll bring you back as soon as the weather's better."

Melvin sipped his coffee, craned his head and listened

to the wind and rain slapping the camp house.

"I've seen worse," Melvin declared. "Just a little wind and rain, that's all."

"At least go back to the farmhouse," Chad persisted. "Remember when I was sixteen and the water blew out the bridge? And a tree fell on the power lines? Didn't have power here for a week."

Melvin looked thoughtful. "Power goes off around here lots. Can't be helped. It'll be the same at the farmhouse as here. No difference."

There was another reason Uncle Melvin preferred the camp house over the farmhouse, but Chad didn't bring it up. Right now, he was more worried about his elderly uncle alone with a major ice storm approaching. But he couldn't push it. "That was the year I killed my first buck," Chad said, forcing a light tone. "Remember?"

"Yep." Melvin's head craned to listen to the wind, which had gained force. "I remember more about what happened twenty years ago than what happened yesterday."

"I remember everything," Chad said. "The way the buck was slipping out behind that doe. I saw that buck before it saw me. Like magic. That buck appeared just like a ghost. Never saw it until it moved its ear." He gave a soft chuckle. "I got so excited I nearly forgot to take the safety off my gun. You remember how long it took us to get that buck out of the swamps?"

"Not really," Melvin said, and gave him a tight grin.

"We've brought so many bucks out from the swamps; it's hard to remember the time it took. But I *do* remember you being excited."

"Well, *I'll* never forget. It took most of the day. Remember, when we got back to the camp, the power was off, and the flood washed away the bridge? If it hadn't been over the Christmas holidays, I could have missed a week of school." He took a deep breath. "I guess that reminded me. I thought it might be a good idea for you to come back with me until the weather gets better. So why don't you think about it? Just till the storm's out'a here."

"Oh, I'll manage," Melvin said. "I like hunting in this weather, especially when I'm fixin to do some serious hunting."

"Still after that old ghost-buck?" Chad asked, eyes crinkling in a smile.

Melvin wasn't offended by Chad's obvious mirth. Chad hadn't seen the buck Melvin talked about either. If he had, the news would have been all over the county. After years of Melvin's stories, folks who knew him believed the buck was a fantasy that only lived in Melvin's mind. Melvin was sympathetic, though. Given the evidence, he'd have thought the same thing. He had no answer when some hunters told him things like, "Well, if it's true, why not just get it with a rifle?" He knew his quest to get close enough to kill with a longbow and a flint arrowhead was nearly impossible. Still, he held his ground.

Lately, Melvin had some misgivings about killing the buck with a longbow and the flint arrowhead he'd found at his ground stand. Maybe the wise old buck would never get foolish enough to be killed with a bow. But, Melvin would do it his way, or no way. Partly because of that, Melvin stopped talking about the buck a few years back. Now, he only spoke about it with Chad.

"Yup, never hunted a buck like this," Melvin replied. "I won't be satisfied until I get him. He knows when I'm around. Every now and then, he lets me get a glimpse. Smart *and* sensible that old boy is. I've never taken this long to get a buck, but don't worry . . . the time's coming. And when I get 'im . . . it will be with my bow."

Chad didn't disagree; he knew better. Once, he saw Uncle Melvin bark-shoot a squirrel at fifteen, maybe twenty paces with his longbow. A bark shot killed the animal without breaking the fur. Chad knew the impact of an arrow wasn't the same as a bullet. Uncle Melvin even marveled at the shot he made. But now, the big buck had become an object so prized, Melvin kept it hidden except at rare moments like this, when he talked about it to someone who had pledged not to reveal what he said.

For his part, Chad didn't talk about the big buck, apart from discussing the prized animal with Melvin, and then only when Melvin brought it up.

Chad was allowed to take clients and friends to hunt on the farm, but they couldn't go into certain areas. His uncle had taken a topography map and outlined the prohibited areas, as if something bad would happen if the territory he'd forbidden was violated. Only Chad could hunt in the banned areas, and only then with a rifle or shotgun, but he chose not to hunt in them.

"Tell you what," Chad said with a grin. "You put me in the place you've been seeing him, and I'll end it once and for all."

"You reckon?" Melvin asked with a half-smile. This was an ongoing joke between them. Melvin believed the buck had earned the right to be hunted on his terms, and in his own habitat, by an old rundown hunter like him. A few weeks back, Melvin told Chad it wasn't the killing—that was of little importance—but that in each man rests a hungry lion. True, Melvin missed the sweetness in the kill. He had wanted to kill several bucks with his longbow over the course of several years. To fight off the urge took willpower. To him, a man's self-control weathered better with age. He didn't want to spoil the hunt taking an inferior buck with the flint arrowhead he'd found. But his determination to kill the monster buck with his bow had wavered some.

Chad leaned forward. "You'll get him sooner or later. Why not take a break and let the weather blow out? You've always told me that bucks stay hid . . . or heck, don't even move when it's raining hard, or it's windy and cold."

Chad got up from the table, walked over to the sink and rinsed his hands, more for something to break the tension than anything else. Then he walked over to the bedroom door, leaned back on the doorjamb, and folded his arms. "Anyway, he's probably several miles from here. Why haven't I seen that big boy? I'd drop him right where he walked."

"Oh, he'll move around all right," Melvin said. "He knows I'm hunting for him. He likes to aggravate me, tempt me. He dares me with his antlers."

Chad made himself a cup of coffee and returned to the table. As he took the first slow sip, the tin on the porch roof banged and rattled in the wind. "I gotta fix that racket," he said. "I'll fix it right now." He slugged another sip of his coffee and they rose to walk outside, Melvin silent but with a curious expression on his face.

Chapter 3

The moment they walked out the door, a blast of wind blew the baseball hat off Chad's head, and his thick blonde hair puffed up before settling down. Tiny raindrops whirled and seemed to float in the porch light. Tree limbs twist and lean in the faint illumination.

Chad grabbed up the hat and jogged to his truck, opened the door and got in the cab, then drove around to the corner of the porch where the tin was loose. After crawling into the truck's bed, he hoisted a concrete block up and tossed it on the tin, then positioned the block so it wouldn't slide off. The weight of the concrete block worked like magic. The current blew a freezing gust, but the tin didn't bang or flap up.

Chad let the tailgate down, hopped off the truck and bounced up the steps onto the porch. "That'll do it," Chad said, and Melvin, no longer curious, nodded in agreement with a proud grin in his face.

They sat across from each other again, and Chad rubbed his arms with the palms of his hands and took a deep breath "Damn, it's cold. I can't believe you're going to stay here. Why not go up to the main house?"

"I'm fine," Melvin replied, and they returned inside the camp house. Melvin walked to the sink and spread apart the stained light-brown curtains that hung limply over it. After peeking out the window, he leaned against the countertop and folded his arms. "I had just about figured out the way that buck worked into his bedding area, *and* the way he traveled to his feeding area . . . at least, until the weather got bad. Rutting season's getting close now, though. Once he starts in rut, there's no telling where he might show up."

The wind gusts plowed through the trees, and Melvin turned to listen. "I don't want to remain in his territory during rut. This buck's too unpredictable. Unnatural. That's why I gotta get him now before he goes in full rut."

"Well, he's gotta change *his* tactics, too," Chad said. "With this bad weather and all."

"Sometimes that monster stays just out'a my range," Melvin said. He whirled around, raised his hands above his ears and spread out his arms and fingers, gesturing like he had a set of antlers.

"That buck will lift up those rocking chairs in a spiteful way and glare at me." He lowered his hands down to his side, frustration evident on his wrinkled face.

"Other times, he'll act as if he doesn't see me, and then he'll maneuver and find a tree between him and me. Like he knows I have one arrow, and he's daring me to take my best shot."

He turned to the window again, thinking.

Chad chose to stay quiet.

Melvin prided himself on killing efficiently, without causing the animal any suffering. To him, maiming an animal was terrible. He'd become highly skilled at instinct shooting—a task not easy to master from various angles. In fact, instinct shooting with his longbow was all he practiced. He'd put himself in various positions and draw and release the arrow from different angles, from standing up to kneeling and back, drawing and releasing the arrow in one fluid motion all through each shift in position. Shooting to his right without turning his body was the most difficult shot to make. He wasn't that accurate at such an angle. But he practiced and practiced until, from sixty steps, he could plant six arrows in a phone book.

As Chad had done only minutes before, Melvin turned the spigot on and rinsed his hands, shook them in the sink and wiped his palms on his shirt. Only then did he lean back against the countertop and look at Chad.

"Sometimes that buck looks like he's thinking, figuring out things. Other times, it's like he's waiting to see what move I'll make. When I make a move, he counters my move by leaving through the opposite end of the area. I make another change by getting into my spot well before daylight. Then, he waits until midmorning before he appears. He makes a move, then I counter his move. It's a hunt I'm enjoying, but . . . he's proving to be the better opponent. So far, at least."

"One day you'll corner him, Uncle Melvin. I'm sure of it. Then you'll clip 'im."

Chad's encouragement was welcome, but Melvin didn't let it show.

"Sometimes I believe that buck's waiting to corner me, get me in a bind. But that's all right. One day he'll overplay his hand. Sooner or later he's bound to make a mistake and *that's* the day it'll be over for 'im."

"Yelp." Chad said with a cautious smile. "That's why I'd take a rifle with me. He'd do that just one time if I had my rifle. I'd clip him."

Melvin shook his head, his eyes distant. "I'm too old to get into the places I should be to mix it up with him. But that's why I've got to stay here. In weather like this, the odds are in my favor. I'm not mad at deer like I used to be. But *this* buck . . . well, that's another issue. I'm mad as hell at him, and I believe he has nothing but contempt for me." Another headshake, then one more.

"This weather is perfect for me to get 'im."

Chad unfolded his arms on the table and leaned back on the bench "Uncle Melvin, you might be right, but . . . the creek's coming up fast. Don't you think the swamp bottoms will be flooded by morning?"

"Not all of it. There's a place that'll be above the flats. About seventy-five acres that won't be covered with water. The water would have to rise higher than ever before to flood that island." Melvin began moving restlessly, gesturing with his hands. "If the water keeps on rising, that old buck might be there. He'll think that island is *his* island, and I'm the trespasser." Melvin was quiet a moment, then said, "Don't think I ever mentioned it before, but I made a ground stand there, near that big oak. You know the one—it's near the oak tree that fell across Narrow Gap Slough."

Chad scratched his chin. "You mean the log at the bottom of that steep ridge?"

"Yelp. That's where I'll be—on that island—if the weather improves tomorrow. Or I might stay on top of the oak ridge. Could be either spot." Melvin nodded toward the kitchen window. "I'll wait and see what the weather's doing in the morning."

Chad looked at his uncle, worried. "That island will flood first, Uncle Melvin. It's low. That's the last and probably worst place to hunt in this weather. It's nearly underwater now, I guess. Check out that map you gave me."

"Yeah, and I know the map's wrong about that. It's a little higher than the flood plain map shows. And I don't care what you heard on the radio: I'm betting the rain will move out tomorrow, probably by morning, early afternoon at the latest." Melvin looked back at his nephew, his gaze steady. "There *is* one thing you can do."

"Sure."

"Tell anyone who's interested I'm okay, and not to worry 'bout me. I have plenty of food, water, coats, warm clothes, propane and candles. Plenty of wood. It's not like I haven't been out in the weather like this before. Should the bridge blow out, I'll be comfortable." He grinned. "Just like you was when *you* got stuck here. So don't worry."

Chad glanced down at his cup, then back up. "So

there's no hope of you coming back with me?"

"It's the best time for me to kill that monster."

"But if the water blows out the bridge, it could be five or six days before anyone can get back in here. That's what I worry about, Uncle Melvin. Something happening and you not able to get help. If you fell down and hurt yourself, or if you couldn't make it out of the swamps, you know those coyotes or wolves could eat you alive. We wouldn't find enough of you to bury! That's the same thing you've told me yourself when I stayed here over Christmas. And be damn sure I don't wanna be the one to discover pieces of you spread all over the bottoms. I'd never get over it."

Melvin grinned, but his tone was resolute. "Only three ways for a hunter to die, and that's just before the hunt, during the hunt or right after the hunt. But you're right about the coyotes and wolves. Only thing in the swamps that spooks me."

"Yeah, you told me that," Chad said, leaning forward. "And sometimes when they're yelping and baying at night, it spooks me too. It's like they're calling to ancient spirits or something. I'd hate to get lost and hear 'em howling. That'd give me the creeps. Remember when you told me the Creek Indians believed coyotes and wolves had big medicine?"

Melvin's face lightened. "Yelp."

"And I don't blame 'em for being mean. They have a hard life. Can't imagine hunting down my groceries with my legs and my jaws. I'd have been a goner a long time ago."

28

"You and me both," Melvin agreed with a chuckle. "But wolves and coyotes are a necessary nuisance. Yeah, they get into chicken coops, kill family pets, slaughter young deer, kill turkeys and eat their eggs. Coyotes kill and eat anything that didn't eat them first. They'll even go after road kill. But they're just doing what nature programmed them to do."

Melvin, in his own way, admired the lowly coyotes and developed an appreciation for their hunting skills. Coyotes kept the field mice down, kept the raccoons out of the corn when it grew. Unlike others, he never saw the coyote as a coward, or even as an opportunistic animal like buzzards, but as an animal that kept the swamps clean of dead animals, and weeded out the weak and the lame. A *necessary* animal, like sharks in the sea. Their population had decreased over the past decade, because every hunter who saw one shot him. Chad had killed several coyotes over the years, too, but stopped when Melvin insisted.

As Melvin spoke, Chad looked at the back door, listening to the wind. By the time Melvin finished, he was looking at Melvin and grinning. "Necessary nuisance, huh? I reckon."

"How's Little Mike doing?" Melvin asked eager to change the subject.

Chad's face brightened. "Oh, *he's* fine. But Beth and me are in a big argument about buying Mike a BB gun for Christmas. You know how she is about him hunting and having a gun." Chad leaned forward a bit more. "Uncle

Melvin, the way she carries on, you'd think I was buying him a three-inch 12-gauge magnum shotgun, a 30.06 *and* a 270 high-powered rifle. He's eight years old, for chrissake! Plenty old enough for a BB gun."

Chad shot up from the table, looked out the back door, then turned back to Melvin. "Last night I told her she needs to get over it, because my son was growing up to hunt and to fish, and Santa Claus would bring him a BB gun this Christmas. Now she's slamming doors and tossing things around, cuts me off whenever I try to talk to her." He snorted. "You know what she said to me the other day?"

"What's that?"

"She said it takes a cruel and cold heart to kill a deer. We got into an argument." He folded his arms and leaned against the pine-paneled wall. "You remember when you let me store my mounted deer head at your house, and then brought it over to my house for me to hang up in the great room?"

"Yep," Melvin replied. "I was meaning to ask you what happened to it. Didn't see it last time I was there."

"I had to get rid of it last month because she *wasn't having a stuffed animal in her house*." His mocking tone gave way to regret. "I gave it to an antique dealer."

His voice was still soft, but Chad's face showed his anger pretty well, Melvin thought. "That's a pity," he said. "Your first buck and mount gave away."

Chad unfolded his arms and strode back to the table.

"Come to think about it, I've never asked why *you* never had a mounted deer head. God knows you've killed some wall hangers."

"Nope, never have."

"Why?"

"To me, deer mounts don't capture a buck's . . . what's the word I'm searching for? Sometimes my mind just gives up." Melvin threw his hand up in frustration. "Don't get me wrong. Makes no difference to me what a man does with his deer. Once, your Aunt Martha and me went to the Atlanta Zoo. I hated it. Animals are too peaceful, too serene in a zoo. Only place I've ever seen real peaceful and serene has been on the face of the dead. A deer mount just degrades the, the . . . magnificent, that's the word I was looking for. A deer mount just degrades the animal's *magnificent* spirit. But it still makes no difference to me either way. It's just the animal's hide pulled over a form. Some folks like 'em, that's all."

Chad looked at Melvin, his grin making his face look boyish. "Well, if you get this ghost-buck, will you mount it?"

"Mount it!" Melvin gave a harsh laugh. "I'll keep the antlers, but to mount that old boy would disgrace him. Can't imagine that old boy wanting to hang over a fireplace."

"If that buck's as big as you say, then it'll be a world-record whitetail buck. People will wanna see it."

"A world record?" Melvin said quietly. "I don't care about that. Only *my* record."

Chad nodded. "I think I know exactly what you mean." At that moment, he decided to stop bugging Melvin about leaving the camp house tonight.

Just then, the front door swung open, and light rain whirled and waltzed around in the porch light and into the kitchen. Chad got up and hurried to close it, but stopped in mid-push. "Hey, look at that wind. I can't remember it being like this." Lightning blinked, illuminating the woods. He watched for a few moments, then closed the door. As he did, the sky rumbled like a bowling ball tumbling down an alley, rattling the camp house's windows.

Melvin walked over to the heater, stooped down and turned the valve slowly. "Yep, the wind is from the northwest. It might get rough tonight. But it'll probably settle down late, and the rain will probably blow out by morning. This weather's been building for four days, it's just now at its peak. It'll pass."

Chad nodded, and then said matter-of-factly, "One more thing, then I gotta go before Flat Creek floods over the bridge. Herman came by and wants to borrow a couple of hundred dollars." He paused, but Melvin said nothing, so he cleared his throat and continued. "I know you've known him a long time, I just don't believe it's good business to keep loaning him money."

As Chad talked, Melvin smiled inwardly. For all the years he'd known him, Herman was always down on his luck. Melvin had hired and fired him dozens of times. He'd come in to work drunk, or he'd walk off a job in the middle of it because things didn't go right. Herman was a World War I vet like Melvin, but a disabled one—he'd been gassed—and always had lots of health problems. Herman got a small VA pension along with his wife's Social Security, but there was never enough money. Melvin felt sorry for Herman, and always did what he could to help him out if it was at all reasonable.

Melvin unfolded his arms and looked at Chad a few moments, thinking about what he was going to say. When he spoke, his words were calm and even. "Give 'im the money. He always pays me back, even if it's a dollar a week. Even if he can't make the full payment, he'll come by and tell me he can only pay a quarter that week."

"Well, I told him I'd consider it," Chad said, "but when I said our company wasn't a bank, he got pissed and called me a runny-nose brat. I wanted to deck him. To be honest, it was painful for me to hold my temper. Then Herman said he wanted to talk with *you*."

"He did?" Melvin said, concerned because Herman wasn't a name-caller.

"Was he drinking?"

"I . . . I don't know."

"Oh, you'd a known if he was. Then again, he probably said that because he *was* drinking, and don't believe you have any dents or been scraped up like a car fender to earn your position."

To Chad's confused look, he explained. "Folks like

doing business with a man that have a few dents here and there. That's where respect comes from. Loan him the money, but tell him I'm not available."

"Okay," Chad said in a way Melvin had learned wasn't okay. "I'll find him when I get in this evening and give that riled-up old fart the money. I *will* tell him no more money for a long, long time. That this is it."

A long pause, then Melvin said, "I trust your judgment. And I know you'll handle it right. You got to be nice to everyone—to a loser, a janitor, or a president of a big company. Treat 'em all the same. Folks like being treated with kindness."

"I've always used that policy," Chad said. "That's the first thing you taught me." He caught himself. "I know it was stupid of me to lose my temper like that. Think I should apologize?"

"Don't worry 'bout it," Melvin replied. "He probably doesn't even remember what he said. Everything going all right with our business?"

"Well, business is good. Maybe too good. All our jobs are coming in on time. Got a big contract for furnishing all the concrete blocks for a new school and gym. Plus, we got all the grading and pipe work. I've have ten or twelve bids out. We're waiting to hear back on 'em. But this weather will keep us down for at least a couple of weeks, maybe more. We'll wait and see."

Melvin nodded. "Keep it up, and don't forget—Oh,

never mind."

"What, Uncle Melvin?"

"It's not important," Melvin replied. "It's your business. By the way, that hundred acres along the lane that leads to the oak ridge?"

"Yes, sir."

"After hunting season, could you bring some equipment here and burn off the broom sage? Oh, and push down all those saplings. Pile 'em up and burn 'em in Gresham's Field. I'd like to cultivate that field and see it grow again." He couldn't bring himself to say the rest of what he'd planned to say: *Your Aunt Martha loved looking across that field when she was alive. I shouldn't have let it get growed up like that.*

"Sure I can do that," Chad said, "but I remember when you retired, you said every day is like a Saturday. You didn't wanna do nothing but relax. And that's the way I think it should be. Can't wait until *I* retire."

Melvin grinned. "Yep, when you first retire, every day is like a Saturday. Then after a few years go by, every day seems like a Friday. And after a few more years . . . every day feels more like a Monday."

"Don't believe I've heard it put that way," Chad said, musing. "You stay active. And you seem to enjoy yourself. But you stay away from folks too much now. Last week at Milly's Café, one of your buddies—can't remember which one—was wondering where you'd been. The guy said, 'No one's seen him around much. Catch a glimpse of him here and there, but he's always in a rush to go nowhere."

As Chad spoke, Melvin went to the sink and rinsed out his coffee cup, then placed it on the countertop. When Chad finished, Melvin leaned against the countertop with folded arms. "Yup, whoever said that was right. I don't know if I have the patience like I used to with my friends. They talk too much about politics, grandkids, about being on fixed incomes and barely surviving. Another thing, too. Several of them used to be strong as bulls, and now they're in wheelchairs from strokes. I'll admit it, it saddens me. So I stay up here where I'm happiest, and I really don't mind it one bit because it's a safe distance. I've got so used to being by myself that when I go someplace—even to the grocery store or for gas—I feel sorta out'a place."

"I understand," Chad said, though he didn't. "And oh, yeah . . . two of our hands just got drafted into the Army. They say a war's coming somewhere in Southeast Asia. Place called Viet Nam. If I was younger and wasn't married, I'd consider joining myself."

For the first time since Chad came in, Melvin tensed. He filled a small glass with water and took a swallow, moved the limp curtains and peeked outside a moment, then turned back and leaned against the counter. "Let me say this, you don't wanna see no war. You're thirty-one years old, and war is for young men. You're too old, Chad. And besides, you won't even get drafted because of the head injury."

"I know, that's why they classified me 4F a long time ago." Chad sighed. "I would've liked going into the Army and serving my country."

"You can serve your country by paying your taxes on time and taking care of your family," Melvin said, hearing but not caring about the snap in his voice. "War is a serious, deadly business. You don't wanna see no war. There's nothing good about war. A lot of my friends were killed in World War I and World War II, and some of our hands who went into the Korean War didn't come back either."

"I remember that," Chad replied, nodding. "I guess I can see why you're no fan of war. Well . . . it was just a passing thought."

Even without turning up the propane stove again, the room had warmed considerably. *Good*, Melvin thought. *The longer it's above freezing outside, the longer Chad can stay. And he needs to hear this.* "I'm glad that's all it is . . . just a thought," Melvin said, his voice rising again. "Those boys you know that go to war? Take a good look at them before they leave, and if they make it back, look in their eyes. You'll see what I'm talking about. War takes the best sons, the best friends, the best husbands. Only the best of everything. Even if you're lucky enough to come back from a war, nothing will be the same again. War robs the innocent and breaks a mother's heart."

Chad saw that Melvin was upset, and gave him a chuckle followed by a reassuring smile. "Well, there's no danger of me getting drafted. Remember? You just said I'm too old."

Melvin knew Chad had tried to join the Marines right out of college, but his football injury kept him out. A lot of Chad's friends had served, though. Once, Chad tried to express to Melvin how much he'd missed out on by being kept out of the military. *"I feel like half a man,"* Chad had moaned. *"Most of my friends are already finished with their tours of duty!"* Remembering his nephew's anguish, Melvin was still afraid Chad would try to fool the Army doctors and join up.

"Promise me you won't." Melvin hated begging, but his order came out like a plea.

Chad looked at the door a moment, and then stared up at the ceiling before turning his gaze to Melvin. "'Kay. I promise. Scout's honor."

Still not satisfied, Melvin walked to the heater and leaned down to shut off the valve, his mind working. "If the weather cooperates, it'll probably take a month for you to clear that hundred-acre field. I'm considering planting it with corn. Maybe some millet and sorghum for game. That ought'a draws lots of quail and doves for you and your friends to hunt. What ya' think?"

"Yep," he said. "I can send some hands up here, and they'll get on it as soon as they can. If some of these jobs hit, it might take longer. But let's see what happens. You see any reason why we can't go ahead and burn off the broom sage as soon the weather dries out?"

As Melvin hoped, Chad sounded a bit more cheerful. "Sounds fine," he said with a nod. "I'll leave it up to you."

Chad stretched out his arms, yawned wide and said, "Wonder if there's any truth to that bullshit story about Gresham's Field?"

Melvin looked at Chad for a moment. "Yelp. Believe it's *alllll* true."

Chad returned Melvin's smile. "Damn! Living back in those days was tough, but how did they know that Aunt Martha's Great-Great-Grandfather Gresham killed that man in that field?"

Melvin looked thoughtful. "I don't know. But hear to tell it—and I've heard several different versions—he *did* kill a man."

"I've heard that, too, but I don't believe Old Man Gresham killed that man just because he was picking cotton at night and stealing a little cotton out of his shed."

Gone now was Chad's regret over not being able to join the military. Now, his earnest face showed doubt. "Gotta be more to that story than all the baloney I've heard."

"Well, to be honest, I believe there's more to that story too," Melvin said, returning to the kitchen table. "When Old Man Gresham killed that man, he let him lay in the field for two days and one night before he let the man's family come over to get the body."

Chad looked at his uncle. "Yep, heard the same thing. That's why I think it's got to be more to the story than him getting mad and gunning the man down."

Melvin reached up and rubbed his forehead. "Maybe so. That man's sons were away, working as tenant farmers several counties over. When they heard about their father being shot dead for stealing cotton, they didn't believe it either. So after the funeral, they went hunting for Gresham. When they found him in the dry goods store hiding behind a cracker barrel, they shot up the whole store. They got Gresham, but a stray bullet killed a little blonde girl walking on the boardwalk right outside the store. Hear tell it, the next day a bunch of townsfolk hunted down those poor boys and lynched them at that old oak tree by the lane right here on the farm. It was a shame. One of those boys they lynched wasn't involved. The young man that *was* involved skipped out during the night, never heard from or seen again. A good thing, because they'd probably have lynched him, too." Melvin gave Chad a wink. "Guess that's the thing about vigilantes . . . they can only be fifty percent right. Like I said, my guess is there's more to the story than what we've been told."

"Is that why they named the field after Old Man Gresham?" Chad ran his hand through his hair and looked up at Melvin.

"Don't know," Melvin said. "Never really thought 'bout it much. But it's a pretty field."

Chad rubbed his hands together. "It sure is! Not a

prettier hundred acres in the entire state. Wonder who planted those oaks to divide the field right down the middle like that?"

"I don't know, but it works," Melvin said, nodding. "I look forward to seeing all the fields planted."

"Well, I'd best go," Chad sighed. "Gotta run some errands before I go home. You sure you don't want to come back with me? I'll worry about you until I see you again."

The old man shrugged his shoulders. "Naw. And I'm not being stubborn or foolish. This really *is* the best time for me to kill that old buck. Any other time I'd say sure, let's make tracks."

"All right, by the way, I brought some groceries and a few snacks for you." He nodded toward the bag on the table. "Oh yes, I forgot to tell you about that old canoe. Don't think about using it. It's got a hole the size of your hand close to the front of it."

Melvin's eyes narrowed. "What happened?"

"I cracked it on the bottoms. I cut out the sheet metal to patch it, but it's still at the shop. Just never got around to it. I was going to come back to repair it, and forgot about it until just now."

"Glad you told me." Suddenly, Melvin didn't want him to go. "What's your hurry, Chad? Stay a little longer and let's talk. Better yet, stay and let's hunt tomorrow."

Chad shook his head. "I can't. I gotta go to Pensacola

in the morning. Beth has to see her mother every other weekend. You *know* how she is about that." He folded his arms and huffed. "What do you think about a woman who wants to spend an entire day with her mother twice every month? Not once, *twice*!"

"Hmmm, I don't know," Melvin said softly. He didn't disagree with twice-a-month visits to *anyone's* mother, but decided it better to say nothing more. Melvin, a hunter, pretty much stayed on Beth's bad side.

"I don't know either," Chad said. "Can't figure her out. But if I can make it back here tomorrow evening, I will. It depends on how long we stay in Pensacola. And if the bridge holds up. If it's gone, I won't be able to come in here." With a sigh that sounded too old for his thirty-one years, he added, "Guess I ought to get going."

Chad stood and stepped over the bench, and they walked out on the porch. Melvin didn't want to, but he found himself babbling now. "It's really coming down now! Look at it rain! It's turning into ice, and look—a snowflake! It's been a long time since I've seen a pretty snowflake." Finally, he stopped himself and turned to his nephew. "Be careful driving out, Chad. See ya when you come back."

Chad moved off the porch and toward his truck. "Hope you get that buck and have him hanging up when I get back."

"Me, too! Tell all hello."

"Will do." Chad turned around and grinned. "And don't

let the wolves and coyotes get into the camp house tonight."

"Okie Dolkie. And hey, tell Herman I'll catch up with him in a few days."

Chad nodded. "If I get bogged down in that ole mud hole, I'll honk my horn."

"'I'll listen out. Be careful."

Melvin stood on the porch and watched Chad drive down the lane, the cold wind pressed against his face. *If only Martha and me could have had kids,* he thought. *If we could have, I'd have been proud to have five sons as fine as Chad.*

Some things, he knew, were not to be. Even so, he refused to put the ghost-buck into the category of things he could never have.

Chapter 4

He went inside and closed the door behind him, then looked at the grocery bag Chad had left. *I forgot to say thank you. I'll remind myself next time I see him.*

He would have liked for Chad to stay longer. The only man alive he really talked with now was Chad. But running the business and his other family obligations prevented Chad from hunting as much as he wanted. Melvin understood, but he knew how much Chad loved hunting and fishing. He didn't believe Chad got enough leisure time.

The grocery bag was filled with canned goods and several packages of deer chops. The canned goods went into the varnished cabinet below the sink. The venison chops, wrapped in brown freezer paper, he placed in the refrigerator. Then he returned to the bench and sat for a while, gazing at the kitchen window.

"A cruel and cold heart," he muttered. "Wonder what Beth knows about a cruel and cold heart." Melvin listened to the wind wailing and continued to brood.

Nature doesn't care about a human heart. Only humans care. Nature is honest, at least. Nature isn't a mother or a father. Nature is an 'it'—and a very old one at that. Nah . . . Nature doesn't get old, only people do. No matter what hand I draw, when it comes time for the showdown, nature will have a royal flush every single time. Some might say the cards are being dealt from the bottom of the deck. But if God is happy with it that way, then I guess I have to be, too.

He allowed himself a chuckle. *You should mind your own business and not think about nonsense, old man.*

Melvin had been angry with God for years; he blamed God for taking his wife. For years, he asked God to give him one favorable sign that Martha was in heaven. That there was a heaven at all. Years later, with no sign, he quit asking God to answer his prayer. It took a long time for him to come to terms with her passing. Many times, Melvin wasn't really sure he ever had.

Martha had helped him get his business up and running. She took care of the books and helped collect money. She was very effective at both. If you saw one, you saw the other; that's what everyone said about them. At forty-five, she got sick. The ovarian cancer took her in a hurry. Melvin was a year older than Martha, and they never had any kids. After Martha passed, a nice home, family and friends seemed not to matter much anymore.

He made himself a cup of coffee and sat back down. He took a sip and rinsed the liquid around his mouth, tilted his chin down and swallowed. Again, Melvin's mind wandered. *If Martha and me could have had kids, I would've wanted my sons to be like Chad. If Chad is happy, then I'm happy, too.*

Melvin never would take any credit for how well Chad turned out. But Melvin believed Chad was mostly unhappy and hated the life he had with his snobby wife. Before Chad married, Melvin warned him that Beth wasn't the kind of woman who could be married to a businessman who worked all the time, and especially one who liked to hunt and fish for relaxation. To this day, every time Chad tried to bring Little Mike hunting with them, Chad would arrive at the camp house alone, reporting that Beth had said no.

Melvin heaved a sigh that came out sounding more like a moan. It would have been better if Chad hadn't talked about his wife that evening.

He glanced at the door, which was moaning with the force of the wind against it. In this weather, he'd never hear Chad's truck horn, and Chad couldn't yell for him. Melvin let the door slam shut as he walked across the porch, stopped and listened, straining to hear a truck horn. All he heard was gusting wind and rain. He was off the porch and into his truck in seconds.

* * *

As soon as he had the gray ''58 Ford running, he turned on the headlights and the windshield wipers, which stuck momentarily before scrubbing across the windshield. After a few more seconds, he drove down the lane to Fannie Road. A short gravel road barely wide enough for two vehicles to pass each other, Fannie Road was maintained by the county and provided the only access to the farm. There was little traffic on Fannie Road, so the county only graded the road twice a year. Melvin never complained about the road's rough condition, or thought about having Chad bring a crew out to work on it. In fact, he liked the road bumpy;

it kept out strangers and kept would-be hunters from trespassing on his farm. Rarely did a hunter trespass on his land, though. Most came and asked permission to quail hunt or dove hunt, and most hunters found him obliging. Except for the off-limit spots, which he carefully showed them on the map.

The three-thousand-acre farm had little road frontage on Fannie Road. The farm's configuration was mostly rectangular, with a large portion of land abutting Flat Creek, which traveled like a crooked snake as it went along the eastern property line. The swamps went the entire length of Flat Creek on both sides. Sloughs, marshes, beaver dams, large oaks and cypresses, among other trees, overran the terrain. The dense vegetation offered plenty of hideouts for turkey and other game. And the ghost-buck.

From the cab of the truck, the slanted silver dashes of falling rain showed up in the headlights as almost solid streaks. Water and mud splashed up as he went through mud holes, and his tires spun. When he arrived at the bad mud hole that had stuck many a truck, he saw that Chad had made it through. He slowly backed the truck onto an old logging road, turned around and headed back toward the camp house.

* * *

Chad was right to worry about the bridge flooding out. Flat River Bridge was a small wood-plank bridge that banged and popped each time a vehicle crossed over it. On still mornings, you could hear a vehicle cross the bridge all the way to the camp house; in fact, you could hear the popping sound from the furthest points of the three-thousand-acre farm. And in rainy weather, there was always the danger of water flooding over the bridge and remaining—sometimes for a day, sometimes much longer.

When Melvin got back to the bridge, he drove the truck onto it, stopped and rolled down his window for a moment, looking and listening to the rushing water. Satisfied, he eased the truck off it.

When he reached the camp house, he fishtailed around to the side of the shed and parked the truck. The shed was a thirty-by-thirty construction of wood planks that had long ago turned gray and dark. In its former life, the shed was a barn used to keep livestock and chickens. Now the shed kept dry all kinds of tools and equipment: a chainsaw, hammer and nails, a vise, fishing poles, coolers, a freezer, shelves, shovels, tackle, plus storage for all kinds of equipment and junk. It also housed a prized 1945 Harley Davidson, something he and Martha used to ride around the farm and on the back roads in the county. The shed's walls provided protection against the wind: not much of an issue most days in South Alabama, but in freezing weather, it could make the difference between a truck that cranked and a truck that wouldn't.

He turned the engine off and clambered out, rushed to the back steps and went up onto the porch. When he exhaled, his breath boiled in his face. He thought how the cold kept animals pinned down. *No animal travels much in*

bad weather, except maybe a rabbit. Poor rabbits . . . every
animal in the swamps and hills want to kill and eat them.
I'd hate to be a rabbit.

He looked at the thermometer tacked on a small piece
of faded plywood—32 degrees. Doing a quick calculation,
Melvin believed the temperature had fallen at least ten
degrees since the sun went down. He glanced back at the
truck, which he could see in the porch light. Judging by the
thin layer of ice on top of the cab, Melvin knew the freeze
had just begun.

Chapter 5

When Melvin went into the kitchen, he looked at the floor and wondered why it seemed to pump up in one spot. With his right foot, he forced his weight down on the vinyl. The floor flexed and depressed. He went to the refrigerator, reached on top and took a small notebook, scribbled something on it and put it back with the same level of detachment as when he looked at the floor.

He moved around the cabin like a robot for a few minutes, flipping the light switch on in each room, as if he were checking or searching for something. He closed each door, jiggling the doorknobs. The power made the lights shimmer and blink off several times before they steadied. He was glad when they came back on and remained on. As he made his rounds, the wind gusts shook the trees, and the fat raindrops made the tin roof hum.

Next, he took an old towel to wipe and dry the floor where rainwater had come in when the door opened, then went to the range, lit the eye and put a kettle of water on. While he waited for it to whistle, he sat at the table, folded his arms, and stared in silence into space.

Melvin had chosen solitude and the easygoing lifestyle that best suited him. He never looked back and wished he'd done things differently. The hopeful and inspired never asked for new cards if their hands didn't pan out. He never thought about winding the clock back. Mostly, he played the hand he was dealt without many gripes. No, being alone on the farm didn't bother him.

The one thing that ran off and hid like a wild animal was conversation. He missed it a lot, if not enough to find someone to talk with just so he could talk. Yet the lack of conversation was the worst part of seclusion and isolation. He missed his conversations with Martha, because they could talk all night just about anything, and many times had.

At times on his farm, he would talk quietly to himself, to trees, flowers and to his garden. Melvin remembered he used to talk to a mule plowing fields when he was younger, but he had a habit of looking over his shoulder when he talked to things now. He didn't want to seem like an old fool talking to inanimate objects that happened to be present at the time he had something to say. At times, however, he believed it better to talk to things that didn't talk back.

Newspapers, current events and politics were boring, and didn't matter to him anymore. He'd planned the exact way he wanted things to be when he retired. There would be no telephone or television. He only read a newspaper or listened to a radio when Alabama played football. Some said he'd given up on everything, but they were misguided. He just preferred peace above everything else.

He knew people thought he lived a lonely life—a meager existence isolated on his farm. Chad wasn't the first one who'd brought it up. But, like the Amish, he was misunderstood. No one could know his pleasure and joy, alone with the days and nights, sights, sounds, freshness in the air and memories as his companions. He was alone, but not lonely as everyone thought. Still, he'd let retirement lure him into too much leisure time.

Back when Martha was alive, he never ran out of things to do around the farm. You could see his pride shine in his neat quarter-acre garden, and Martha's rectangular flowerbeds held fountains of rainbows. Now, he had the swamps, large trees with moss, and wide-open fields and smaller fields overwhelmed by sapling trees, broom sage, undergrowth and animals.

On some nights the owls, coyotes, frogs and crickets sang diminutive, wild melodies with broken lyrics. To him, their chorus was flawless. He heard no cheapness or exaggeration in the simple harmonies. Sometimes Melvin would sit on the porch with all the lights off and just listen.

He always said he liked to see colors in a sunrise and sunset, because they never wore out. At night, sometimes, he'd catch a glimpse of a star shooting across the sky, then fading out, and it reminded him of a musical note. These were ordinary things to most, but to him these were priceless moments one couldn't buy or trade. He believed a true hunter saw and felt these kinds of things. And he believed he had discovered a fortune many hunters only dreamed about. Yet he knew those who weren't nature-oriented hadn't the faintest notion about how to see, understand, hear, smell, touch or gain strength from those things a hunter saw in the solitude of hunting. The things he discovered while in the swamps rejuvenated and fit him like a robe on a king.

Money was no worry. He owned the farm outright and he was a rich man, a man of means. But money didn't matter to him anymore. Nothing really mattered much since Martha died.

But, over the past four years, the big buck had become increasingly important in his life. No, it was more than that. He wanted to kill a world-record buck with his longbow and one handmade arrow topped by the Indian flint arrowhead he'd found.

His quest for the big buck gave him something solitude, peace and comfort lacked: a magnificence and sweetness in the thrill derived only from the hunt. Only a hunter could understand his passion. If the time ever arrived when he couldn't experience or feel the hunt, it would be the end. But not a fitting end for a true hunter.

On more than one occasion, he had been tempted to take his rifle and kill the buck. Every time, he'd been nearly out of sight of the cabin before he returned and put the rifle up.

He knew another hunter might kill the trophy with a rifle sooner or later, and he wouldn't blame them. Yet, that wasn't him. To him, there was no dignity in killing the enormous buck with his rifle. He wanted to kill it with a thousand-year-old weapon used by great hunters. He wanted to hunt like the Great Plains Indians, Cherokees, and Creek Indians did. He wanted to kill the buck with no treachery and to kill the buck with a bow and arrow. That's why he hunted from a ground stand, and with the most primitive weapon he could handle. He wanted a fitting and honorable kill for what he believed was a king: the king of all whitetail bucks.

For two years, he'd quarreled with himself about taking his rifle, and he soon stopped even taking the rifle to the camp house. It became too much of a temptation, especially after the buck had shown itself to him. He kept a .38 caliber pistol in the camp house for security, but never brought it into the woods. In fact, he hadn't fired the pistol in two years.

When he put limitations on folks about hunting on his farm, it hadn't produced the kind of result he wanted. To him, his limits were reasonable. But, to some folks, Melvin had become odd and ornery. Many thought he'd lost his touch with deer hunting. Others simply believed he was touched because he refused to kill the trophy with his rifle.

Even Melvin couldn't figure out why he'd become so unlucky. Every hunt planned out, yet on each encounter, the buck sunned in victory. When he walked back from hunting, any observer could tell he'd seen the big buck by the way he walked with his powerful shoulders hunched. But the observer didn't know his mind: Each time, Melvin wondered if the buck was just luckier, or if there was something divine interfering and keeping him from taking it.

Although Melvin was a seasoned and experienced deer hunter, he did sense danger with this particular deer. All his years in the swamps and oak ridges, he'd never seen an animal be mean to another animal. Yet he'd seen the big buck rear up on its hind legs and attack another buck, even when it wasn't during rut. He knew how territorial a buck was during rut, but this buck was no ordinary buck. It was a monster buck, a big, mean, king mossback. Mossback was the name he gave the big buck, because the hair on its back was the color of Spanish moss. Even the texture appeared eerily similar.

He'd seen the buck perform other acts that weren't natural for a buck. Once, he saw the buck attack a raccoon and try to trample it. No reason that Melvin could see, either. The raccoon was minding its own business, washing its food in the slough. The raccoon got into the slough before the buck could do any damage, and the buck disappeared in the woods before Melvin could bring himself out of his daze.

What rattled Melvin most was when he saw the buck attack another raccoon. That day, the buck had walked within range of his longbow, a twenty-step, clear-front shoulder shot with his bow. A shot he could have made easily.

Everything happened so fast, he convinced himself he didn't really freeze. He never owned up to it because, to him, it was something that never happened. He was sure he hadn't contracted the dreaded buck fever—what other hunters had described as a living-hell state of mind. Buck fever was something all hunters dreaded, because it immobilized them—froze a hunter so he couldn't shoot, or couldn't shoot straight. One of those fevers only a hunter could become infected with, and from which no hunter was immune. If a hunter got buck fever at the time an angry lion or hungry bear charged, the split-second advantage of the weapon was lost. It meant killing the animal with your bare hands, or the animal killing the hunter stone cold. No, Melvin had never had it happen before, and he shivered at the prospect of getting the fever at the time an aggressive animal was after him.

But what unnerved Melvin more than anything, what might have made him hesitate (*not freeze*) was when he saw the buck's snout the day it attacked that second raccoon. There was an ugly gully that went straight across the buck's snout, like a spoon had scooped it out. Immediately, Melvin knew it was from a gunshot wound. He reasoned that, long ago, someone maimed instead of killed the buck.

He went into every hunt knowing exactly what he was going to do and how. But when he thought about freezing, and even though he wouldn't admit it happened, he became unaccountably infuriated with himself.

In the throes of that anger, he got up from the table and walked to the sink, then pushed aside the faded curtains and shoved his face close until the windowpane fogged.

A lightning bolt flashed across the belly of the clouds. The thunder was instantaneous, so loud that butterflies flew around in his stomach. Melvin shuddered and backed up, blinking, hoping the weather would move on soon.

Chapter 6

He listened to the strong winds push against the camp house and the torrential rain falling. He thought how weather could foul up a hunting, fishing or camping trip, or interrupts a vacation and a man's sleep.

Idle time made him restless, but there was nothing else he could do right now to take the edge off. To pass time, he walked around the big kitchen with his hands in his back pockets, looking at the walls and ceiling, checking the old kitchen window for leaks, wondering if the tin roof would hold through the night, thankful that Chad had taken care of the flapping piece of tin on the porch. A half-hour of pacing, and he became lightheaded. That's when he remembered he hadn't eaten since lunch. He decided to fry some venison and potato with onions. A hearty meal of meat and potatoes would hush the roller coaster in his stomach.

Although he loved to cook, eating had long ago become a chore. *Something about cooking for yourself when you're not hungry affects the appetite*, he thought. *Then, you can't consume all you've cooked.* The plate would be clean tonight, though—the hunger pangs were gnawing at his stomach now.

The kitchen sink had hot water, run from the water heater in the bathroom, but he never used it if he had hot water already in the kettle. He felt the kettle. It was still warm, so he removed it from the stove and poured hot water into the dishpan, took the greasy black skillet and scrubbed it with a hand rag, careful not to remove the seasoned dark coating in the skillet. He used a ragged towel to swab the interior of the skillet, and it was clean.

A small cardboard box on the floor was used to keep potatoes and onions. He took the biggest potato and a tennis ball-sized onion and put them on the countertop, then walked to the refrigerator and opened it. The door made a noise like tape peeling away. *Needs a new gasket*, he thought, but made no move toward the notebook on top of it.

He removed two deer chops from the brown package Chad had brought, then placed the package back in the refrigerator and rinsed the chops in cold water. The action reminded him to let the spigot drip so it wouldn't freeze during the night. He put the lean venison on a platter, took a napkin and pressed the meat dry. Salt and pepper on both sides, then he coated the meat in flour.

He rested the black skillet on the stove and added several tablespoons of bacon grease before lighting the fire under it. He washed the potato and onion, then quartered them with his butcher knife after pulling the peel from the onion. When he placed them in the skillet, they sizzled. He rinsed his hands, shook them in the sink, and wiped his palms on his shirt.

After the onions and potatoes finished cooking, he placed the deer meat in the scalding grease, and then turned down the flame a bit. White threads of vapor rose from the meat and he inhaled, savoring every bit of the aroma that reminded him of the year he learned to cook. His recollection carried him back to Texas.

It was 1916. He'd seen a silent movie about cowboys when he was a kid, so he wanted to be a cowboy one day. As soon as he could, he went to Texas and got a job on a ranch as a cowhand. Being a cowboy was hard, tough work, but he adapted.

When he arrived in Texas, he didn't have a cowboy hat or cowboy boots. The other hands teased him about it, so he used his first paycheck to buy a fine cowboy hat and a pair of hand-tooled boots. Back then, a cowboy could tell another cowboy by the way he walked and by the way he wore his hat: a low brim, a shadow over your eyes. He'd once told Chad that his eyes were a brimful of spring back in those cowboy days.

For several weeks, his work consisted of throwing fifty-pound bales of hay onto a flatbed, or digging postholes until he nearly wore out. After several months, he was riding a horse, looking and feeling like a cowboy: tired all the time.

His first cattle roundup lasted three weeks, and that was where he learned to cook. They ate out of a chuck wagon, and he loved it. The chuck wagon was full of equipment, from ropes to salve for saddle sores. The cowboys demanded plenty of coffee and food, and the old cook showed him how to make stews, steaks, and the best pinto beans in the world.

"The most important man on a cattle drive is the cook," the old fella told him. *"A cook on a cattle drive must be a doctor, a dentist, a barber, a judge and a good listener. Cattle roundup without a good cook raises tensions. Make things so tense, the cowhands start fighting each other, or even stop working."*

Back then, Melvin learned one important thing about being a cowboy: It wasn't permissible to talk during meals, and no-talking was strictly enforced. He came to believe the only time a true cowboy was at peace with himself was at mealtime. Since that first day, he never talked during a meal.

On his first cattle drive, Melvin was allowed to stand watch over a herd of cows, a responsibility not entrusted to just any cowboy. He could remember how serene it was then, even when the coyotes yelped in the night. On that cattle drive, he discovered why a cowboy was a cowboy.

A smile came to his face, thinking about those times in Texas, and the Mexican women. He blinked several times, and his thoughts were gone. Now he was back at the stove in the camp house in the middle of a bad storm and on the trail of a ghost-buck. But everything was still all right; the chops hadn't yet burned.

With the fork he was holding, he flipped the venison over. As he watched the chops blistering to a golden brown, he listened to the arctic gusts and to the rain. The wind through the trees sounded like someone trying to whistle. The rain stopped, then it would start, then it would fall, then slow down like breaks in ocean waves. He could tell the rain coming down wasn't as substantial as before. This made him more confident the rain would stop by daylight. But there would be plenty of ice.

After a few minutes, he removed the venison chops from the bubbling grease and laid them on napkins he'd placed on a platter.

After he finished eating, he cleaned up the kitchen and swept the floor, moving things around and making them neat. As he cleaned the kitchen table, he thought about taking a shower, and then decided against it. He would wait until the morning. He preferred to take a shower in the mornings anyway, if he'd hadn't worked or done anything to work up a sweat.

He wandered over to the sink, splashed cold water on his face, took a towel and scrubbed his face dry. He only shaved once a week, and always on Sunday, a habit he got into right after he retired. In the back of his mind, he'd considered just growing a beard. In his business life he was always clean-shaven, except he did have a brown mustache. A mustache was acceptable. But, for the most part, any facial hair was frowned upon.

Many folks felt anyone who had a beard was antisocial, a nonconformist, a communist who didn't bathe or work, or, in more recent years, someone who didn't love their country. He believed labels were easy to attach to someone, but hard to remove. Yet it was funny; it wasn't a positive asset to have a beard when conducting business, but a moustache was okay. He never saw a banker with a beard *or* a mustache. Once, a business associate told him a banker wouldn't be trusted if he had a beard to hide behind.

Melvin was a trusting man, bordering on the gullible, when he first started his grading and hauling business. He believed taking a man's word was enough. But he discovered it was never good enough. People would beat you out of your money if you gave them a half-chance. When he started his business, he learned fast. Learned he couldn't threaten bodily harm to a man just because the man owed him money. Learned he couldn't threaten a man with criminal action to resolve a civil issue about money owed to him. Learned if another man beat him out of money, he couldn't call him a crook. He nearly went broke four times before he wised up.

Melvin also learned the worth of a dollar. That it was better to take a thousand dollars today than to wait a year to get eleven hundred dollars. That it was better to get the job finished as quickly as possible. That if a man wanted twenty yards of gravel hauled to a specific location at a specific time, the gravel should get there a little early. That if he was supposed to have his equipment on the job at a specific time, it should be there.

As he worked to establish himself in the business world, he observed how lawyers, accountants, engineers and architects dressed and carried themselves. He started wearing starched khakis, nice shirts, nice shoes or cowboy boots. His size-twelve cowboy boots made him look six-foot-three, but no matter what shoes he was wearing, he walked in long, measured strides: something he'd learned from being a cowboy. He liked his shirts loose, because a tight fit around his arms made him uncomfortable if he had to lift something. He wore his pants a little baggy for the same reason. His big hands and nails were always clean, especially when he met a customer. When he shook hands, most noticed hard skin but hands that were clean and not scratchy. That was because he wore gloves when he worked. It was Martha who told him he had to start wearing gloves. He protested, but after a month, he went along with it.

There were a few rules he balked at, though. He never wore a tie or a hat to conduct business. He wore a hat only when he worked in the field. But he was always clean-shaven and his thick, chestnut-brown hair always looked fresh. People trusted his green eyes because they were friendly, good-natured, with a gentleness that was honest and humble.

Martha told him his skin looked like tanned porcelain, except for the little scar that went down an inch at the corner of his left eye. First thing people noticed about him was his wide shoreline smile that was contagious and approachable. He smiled, thinking of that. *Contagious* and *approachable* were the very words Martha had used when she tried to explain what first attracted her to him.

When he met a customer, he never made a joke or laughed at a joke told by a customer. To him, money and doing business was no joke. He'd listen to his clients more than he talked. When he showed up to get paid for a job, he got paid for the most part. He was always willing to work with a man, who got in a financial bind, but he always insisted on a signed personal note, and he charged interest for financing. By the time he'd been in the business for a few years, he had unconsciously gained a way to people seeing things his way. If you owed him money, it was always best to tell him you could only pay a certain amount, but you could pay so much money at another time.

Another inflexible rule was he never gave money to anyone to get a job, or to get a job approved. Trusting the wife or a girlfriend of a customer was bad business, too. Once, the wife of a customer offered him her body if he'd knock off some money for the grading job he contracted to do for them. He asked her how a bank would accept sex as payment for the money he'd borrowed to finance the job. Because of that and similar situations, he'd learned that the word "no" was the most important word in business, and probably in life.

In his bedroom, he opened a drawer and put a pair of insulated underwear on top of his washstand. It was too early to go to sleep, so he went back into the kitchen, sat at the table, shoved the coffee cup away and folded his arms. For a while, he sat drumming his fingers on the table, whose ancient, tight-fitted planks were almost silent under his tapping.

Melvin had a way of judging time, and he knew how he'd changed over the years. Now, if he went to bed too early, he was tired the next day, no matter how long he slept. Being tired most of a day wasn't what he wanted. He never really slept or drifted off to sleep while hunting from his ground stand. He knew he snored—Martha was the first one to tell him that—and it was tough enough hunting a deer while quiet. Going hunting when he was tired complicated matters more than that. He became fidgety, restless, and couldn't remain still or comfortable long. Once in his life, he could work an entire day and stay up half the night, then work the next day without getting tired. Those days were gone, and he was glad of it.

There was no one to talk with, and he liked it that way most of the time. For one thing, he wouldn't have to listen to Chad's pleas about not hunting the monster buck because of the bad weather. The last thing a man wants is someone begging him not to do something. A man his age had earned the right to live in peace without any bother from anything or anyone. Yet, he was bothered about what folks were saying about him and the big buck.

Sure, he liked friends or family members stopping by to hunt or visit. He liked it a lot. And he liked to hunt with them, as long as they didn't hunt with a rifle or shotgun in the areas he had prohibited. Some of his friends told him they were either sick or not feeling well, or had decided to quit hunting altogether. He knew better. They didn't want to hunt on the farm anymore because they couldn't hunt where they really wanted. They wanted to hunt in the areas where he'd seen the enormous trophy. The prize they had never seen.

It was his farm, and he didn't give a crap anymore what they believed or said, but the idea that everyone thought it was some fantasy buck *did* hurt. He resented that thinking, because he'd never manufactured a story to impress anyone. They'd seen the kind of trophy bucks he killed in the past with a rifle, and couldn't appreciate why he gave up hunting this buck with a rifle. But he certainly wasn't going to plod through all the reasons why he wanted to kill the big buck with his longbow and the flint arrowhead.

Yet it went deeper than that. The only thing he feared was getting old to the point he couldn't fend for himself. Dependence on someone was in the back of his mind, and he dreaded it. The last thing he wanted was to end up an old man who couldn't care for himself. He preferred death to becoming a burden. He'd seen what old age did, and he wanted no part of becoming dependent or simply tolerated because of his age. He believed in nature taking its course. In that respect, he figured nature was more benevolent than man.

He wandered over to the kitchen window and stared out. Lightning still flared, but more distant now, and he heard brief thunder in the aimless sky. Ice had formed on the tree limbs, making them look like bluish ghosts in the lightning flashes. The sounds made by the storm stirred up all kinds of ideas; thoughts loaded into his mind, and he let them roll.

Nature was peaceful and serene most of the time, but

he saw nature's savage and violent side. A byproduct of surviving, he reasoned. To him, nature wasn't something to play around with, because nature had a way of correcting things, like a determined woman who knows how to get her way.

He understood his own beliefs, but he never shared what he really thought with anyone other than Martha. Besides, who'd listen to an old man? Who would take him seriously unless they understood and felt like he did?

Probably one reason old age has little respect for youth, he thought. *Youth haven't paid its dues; youth sees no end and has no concept of dying or aging. Youth has no worries. Youth lives for the moment. Or for the next day, at most.*

He knew that if he had the chance to turn back the clock, he would probably pass it up. But he still wondered at how fast his early years had passed. When he reached sixty, after Chad was married to Beth, he told Chad, *"One day you wake up, and you wonder what happened to the time. Why does time seem to go faster the older you get? It's like a runner burning out in the hundred-yard dash."*

Chad, being young, had no real answer.

But solitude at his age was exactly what Melvin wanted, not the other way around. He'd had a good life and he knew it. He had economic worth, he was happy; he'd had a good wife, a good business. But hard work, day in and day out, listening to people who couldn't pay on time, customers complaining, employee problems, having to bite your tongue, the whole gamut of running a business had taken the sweetness out of his life after Martha passed.

Running a business is for the young man, not for an old man, he thought. He didn't have the patience he once had and he knew it. When he realized that, it was the day to retire. Now, the quiet and solitude gave him a feeling of everlasting youth. No worries.

Besides, it was better to be on the farm than hanging around Milly's Café drinking coffee every morning with other old men who had nothing better to do than to drink coffee, talk about nonsense, wars and politics. It was like a club after you retired. You'd go to Milly's Café and drink coffee until you had to pee several gallons of water while you listened to men with opinions on every topic in the world that nobody really gave a crap about. Then you had to look at Miss Milly, with her painted-on black eyebrows and unnatural black hair in a beehive and dark red lipstick. Poor lady. At fifty-five, she felt she was still the belle of the county.

No, he had better things to do with his time, and felt lucky he could do them.

It wasn't long after he retired that he convinced himself nature never intended man to stop working. Retiring, to him, was like taking a new car and parking it beneath a tree. After five years, the car wouldn't crank, the tires were flat, the windshield was foggy and the battery was dead. He was determined that wasn't going to happen to him.

After hunting season closed, and if the weather was good, he'd walk around the entire farm, about a mile-and-a-half walk. He carried a crooked oak limb carved into a walking stick with him. Along the path, he would move brush and limbs aside and make mental notes about things he wanted done.

When he took his walks, he looked for Indian arrowheads, deer tracks, old rub on trees made by a buck the previous year, evidence that the big buck was moving around. He tended to his quarter-acre garden, or worked around the farm and on the several outbuildings, and kept things immaculate around the main house.

After he retired, it became more and more work to plant the nine fields on the farm. Four years before, he decided not to plant a single one. The following year, he decided to wait until the next year. Now, nearly all the fields were grown up in sapling trees and briars. This year, he'd have at least one field cleared off and brought back like they were in the past. He couldn't imagine why he let them get in that condition. It was a damn shame.

He still had a lot of things he wanted to do around the farm. Getting the fields back like they once were would keep him busy and make the year pass faster if he didn't get the buck this year.

Every early spring, he went fishing with a cane pole. But not always. He loved fishing with a fly rod and a popping bug for big bluegills, shell crackers and the occasional bass. Sometimes he'd run a trotline for catfish. He never ate catfish—they were bottom feeders—so he gave away nearly all the fish he caught to a black family that lived several miles away. Good people, but they always looked like they could use a helping hand. But fish wasn't the only thing he'd done for them. He owned the land, and essentially gave them a life estate on the property.

Right after he retired, he had a routine, and wasn't sorry about it. When hunting season closed, he'd relax on the porch of the main house and watch the distance, as if he was watching for something to walk out of the horizon. Maybe even then he was looking for the buck, or something like it. Those times, he relished his treasure chest of memories. They were bountiful and rich, and he turned their pages like turning pages in a picture album. They never bored him or put him on a guilt trip, and he could leave them anytime he liked without making an excuse. That was the best part.

He thought about his trips down the Colorado River, and the time he backpacked across the Rockies. The time he lived for a solid month in the swamps, trapping and hunting, just to see if he could survive off the land.

Before Melvin got married he'd been in barroom brawls, was a poker player, a man who'd take a drink, a man who'd never bet a man at his own game, and a man who swore. And he had been to war.

After a while as a cowboy, he got into bull riding and

bronco riding in a local rodeo in Laredo. And he met Cowboy Cody. Cody was a big man from Oklahoma, twenty-five years older than Melvin, and he took a liking to Melvin right away. Cody taught him a lot about being a cowboy, and about Fairbanks, Alaska. How it was nearly like the Old West. "Only difference is the snow," he'd said to Melvin. Cody served in the Spanish-American War, so Melvin could talk to him about his own memories, and Melvin came to love him for that.

One Saturday afternoon in Laredo, Cowboy Cody was thrown from a bull and hit his head on a split rail fence. He died before a doctor could get to him. The closest Melvin came to crying was when he found out that Cowboy Cody's only possessions were his horse, his saddle, a pair of revolvers and his clothes.

When his friend died, Melvin lost his heart about being a cowboy. Not long after that, Melvin started thinking about all the things Cowboy Cody said about Alaska. And that's when he decided to see for himself.

Melvin never again talked about his experiences in war, but he'd seen lots of action in Europe. In a brief battle near the Ourcq River in France, he was bayoneted in the side and shot in the right shoulder. While he was recovering from his wounds at Fort Gordon, Georgia, the war ended, and he was glad. His soft green eyes that once absorbed everything in sight were replaced by tough granite, and his smile was rare. His voice was deeper and his words more careful, wider. He would stop at times, look off, and remain preoccupied until he was interrupted.

The day before Thanksgiving at Fort Gordon, he was walking to the mess hall for breakfast with several other walking wounded. When they entered the mess hall, he breathed in the pungent scent a thawing turkey donates, and it reminded him of human flesh burning in the cold. His awareness was gone in a blink. In that split-second eternity, he became an animal with one thing in mind, and that was surviving. It took six grown men to hold him down.

Since then, he'd never found anything charitable about the scent of turkey. Wouldn't venture into a house when turkey was being roasted. Many thought he was odd about Thanksgiving because he never came around. It didn't matter to him what others thought, but he didn't want to make a fool out of himself and ruin Thanksgiving for everyone else. Besides, being at the camp house or in the swamps hunting was more fulfilling. There, he was no different from any other veteran who'd seen hand-to-hand combat and survived.

* * *

By the time he returned to Alabama, he'd seen and done more than most men would see or do in a lifetime. He did everything else he wanted before he was thirty, the year he married. Before that, Melvin was a man from the wild side. At times like these, on stormy, lonely nights, Melvin often thought about the adventures he had while he was young. It was amazing how fond memories of youth act like a medicine to soothe the mind, and the way a fond memory and things done or learned seemed to hold a genuine smile on the lips or brighten up the mind.

He was fond of one memory in particular. He'd told Chad many stories about his trip to prospect for gold in Fairbanks, Alaska in 1922 and 1923. About the friend he had met in Fairbanks at the Gold Rush Saloon. He was sitting at the bar when a mountain of a man walked in: a black-bearded man so huge he had to turn sideways to enter the door and the biggest man Melvin had ever seen. The man's name was John Swede. John was over six-foot-six weighed about three hundred pounds, and wore beaver hides and pelts. John looked and smelled like an animal, and had one huge belly laugh.

Melvin could still remember what John said when he walked in the Gold Rush Saloon. Waving one huge paw of a hand, John bellowed, "I'm the baddest, the meanest, and the ugliest man in the Yukon. I can out-fight, out-wrestle, out-dance, out-run, out-shoot, out-drink any man alive. I eat bark off trees for lunch and wipe my butt with briars."

Hearing those words again made Melvin smile, and he wondered whatever happened to John the Swede. During World War II, John's once-a-year letters stopped coming, and Melvin didn't try to find out why. He was afraid to know.

A loud, sustained gust hit the kitchen window and brought the *rat-a-tat-tat* of sleet. He felt a strong draft and heard it groan, but the window held. Best he get his hunting equipment ready, just in case his intuition was right and the weather broke by morning. Amazing at times how intuition seemed the better judge about most things. *"Intuition is a graceful lady,"* he often remarked.

His notion that the weather was going to improve made him eager, restless. It rarely made any difference, though; he could hunt an entire day in the worst weather and be tired as a dog, not sure if he'd go back to hunting the next morning. Just before daylight, he would awaken and be young at heart again. No, he would never miss a day to hunt, no matter the weather. With that in mind, he closed the memory book.

Chapter 7

He looked at the wall where his bow quiver hung. When he walked to it, his shadow slid along the wall. He took the quiver and returned to the kitchen table, then removed the single arrow from it.

He'd made the bow quiver out of beaver hide. It was twenty-eight inches tall, and round, with a six-inch opening at the top. He used round hickory limbs for the frame and to form the pouch. For a price, a local trapper had supplied the beaver hide, which Melvin had stretched and pulled tight around the frame with string. He had inserted cardboard into the interior of the quiver to separate the arrows from the hickory frame. A hawk's tail feather he'd found on the floor of the swamps was tied to the top of the quiver with a piece of twine six inches long.

Melvin eschewed the store-bought shafts and had a local carpenter make several arrow shafts for him, thirty-three inches long to match his draw. The shafts were round and made of white oak, and their circumference was identical to a store-bought wooden arrow shaft. He'd made the fletching himself out of turkey feathers, and carefully carved the notch into the wood to match the diameter of the bowstring.

But all but one of those arrows was put away. The only arrow in the quiver was fitted with a flint arrowhead. It was a beauty: The flint's point was four inches long and two inches at its base. He'd found the arrowhead while building

long, then, at once, letting the air out of their lungs. Restless again, he moved from room to room, looked out the window, poked his head out the door for a minute, just listening and watching. The wind was strong, and he didn't feel particularly safe in the old camp house, but he believed it would endure this storm. After all, it was older than he was and probably survived worse storms than this.

But he was edgy and had a bad feeling: the same kind of feeling he'd gotten before combat in France during World War I. Once you experience the feeling, you never forget it, and he believed the experiences in battle never left a combat veteran.

He was itching for the wind and rain to move on. Alone in a storm didn't bother him, but he felt different. Not afraid, but uneasy, unsettled, a tightening in his stomach. It was times he felt this way that he thought about the buck. It simmered inside him and boiled up once in a while.

The big buck had stalked him out of the swamps on more than one occasion; he was sure of it. If not the buck, then *something*. Whatever stalked him never ventured into the open so he could see it. The closer to rutting season, the more often he felt the buck slipping up behind him at dark. The buck's unnatural behavior had spooked him on more than one occasion. He felt intimidated leaving the swamp, but he wasn't afraid. No, not afraid.

But he wasn't stupid either. Melvin frequently looked over his shoulders when walking out from a hunt at dark. He was certain the buck—or whatever it was—would ambush him at a moment he was least expecting it. As a precaution, he left the swamps before it got too dark. He didn't want to get mauled in the dark by *any* animal.

Melvin was still surprised he'd ever told Chad about the buck stalking him, especially how it made him feel. It was totally out of character for Melvin to say such a thing. Melvin wondered if Chad had seen that as a sign of weakness, that his uncle was less of a man. But Chad never gave him any sign, just calmly acknowledged the scope of Melvin's apprehensions.

Melvin was ready for a showdown with the buck. The showdown didn't bother him. Instead, it was the uncertainty of when it would come. *That doesn't make any sense*, he chided himself. *I'm not an amateur or novice hunter. The timing of the unexpected shouldn't bother me at all. That's what hunting's all about. If you're ready, it doesn't matter what comes your way, or when. Hunting's not like fishing. You never knew what would take the bait or bite an artificial plug.*

What he didn't want was to be panic-stricken and undone, like the time he froze. He wanted the confrontation on *his* terms, when he was ready and expecting it. He suddenly wondered if a divine power was directing him, leading him toward the path for a confrontation. If so, would he get a second chance to stick the buck? He knew he'd missed his opportunity when he froze.

There, he finally admitted it: He froze. But that was something no one would ever know, even Chad.

For a couple of hours he piddled around and went out on the porch, moved boxes around, cleaned the sink, put dishes up, looked in the bathroom, piled up dirty laundry in a cardboard box for washing at the farmhouse. The storm interrupted his normal routine, but as long as he kept busy, it helped the time to move on faster.

When he ran out of made-up chores, he stood by the table, adjusted his belt, placed his right hand on the table's edge and went down on the balls of his feet, then pushed up until he was straight. Then go down again and back up, until his lower joints complained. Then he walked to his bedroom door, placed both palms on the door and leaned forward, then pushed back until he started to wheeze. *What's the use?* he thought, fighting for breath. *You can remodel an old house, but you can't transform its physical age.*

A flash of lightning lit up the outside, the windows rattled and the lights in the cabin blinked off and on. He cursed softly when he heard the heavy rains begin again. Then, the power went out.

After a few moments, the lights blinked, then steadied back on. He went into his bedroom and located his three-cell flashlight, rested it on the golden oak washstand so he'd know where it was. While he was there, he stared at some old photographs tacked onto the wall. Many of them had faded, especially the colored ones, but most were in black-and-white. It saddened him to see the old photographs, pale with age, especially the ones of Martha.

He kept a photograph of her in his wallet, but could rarely bear to take it out and look at it.

His first smile came when he saw the photograph of him and Bell Starr, and his mind filled with memories of the dog. He'd bred her for deer hunting, and of all the hunting dogs he had had, Bell Starr was the best. She would run a deer for three or four minutes, stop, and then come right back to him. Then she jumped another deer if she found one. Bell Starr was a cross between a bird dog and a black-and-tan. Her nose was keen to the scent of a buck. She'd jump a doe, but she wouldn't run it long. And she wouldn't hunt for anyone except Melvin. A special trust existed between them. Melvin always saved Bell pieces of bacon—her favorite—as a treat, and let her ride in the front of the truck if it was raining or too cold. Sometimes he'd let her ride in the front anyway.

One day when Bell Starr was eight years old, somebody shot her with a rifle. Melvin never knew if the person who shot Bell Starr mistook her for a deer, or what. It didn't matter; whoever shot the dog wasn't a hunter, or a man. *But if I'd found out who shot my dog, they'd have had me to reckon with*, Melvin thought, swallowing the lump in his throat.

He buried Bell Starr beneath a small plum tree within sight of the camp house's back porch. A set of deer antlers marked her grave. Many times, when he started to leave the camp to hunt, Melvin would glance over at it, just to make sure the antlers were still there.

It was Martha who'd named her, but she had died when Bell Starr was still a puppy. Most times, Melvin was glad Martha never knew what happened to the dog.

I bet Bell would find out where that old buck was hiding, he thought, fighting another lump in his throat. *She'd locate that big buck. She'd know right where to go. She knew more about deer hunting than me.* He lowered his head and stared at the floor for a while, not seeing.

It's amazing how a dog knows people better than people know people. An animal's love is pure, no reservations. The kind of love that some say is probably close to God's. I bet she has the wings of an eagle now.

He would've liked to have several dogs and cats around. Even a yard dog was better than no dog at all. But after Bell Starr was killed, the other dogs he'd had never made it on the farm. They would disappear, or die. He had a puppy he named Big Joe, but Joe was only a year old when he was attacked one night near the camp house by either a pack of coyotes or a big wildcat. Melvin heard the fight, but didn't make it in time. Whatever attacked Big Joe tore him to pieces. House cats especially never had a chance, because of the wild animals. Something would eventually track them down, kill and eat them. When a cat came up missing, they were seldom, if ever, seen again. Once, he saw a big owl fly down and grab a small kitten. Raccoons and opossums were notorious for killing all the housecats they came across. Coyotes never missed an opportunity to take out a housecat either.

It was suddenly hard to breathe in the bedroom, so he went through the kitchen and out on the porch. Leaning against the rail, he breathed in the cold and watched the rain splashing. The individual drops seemed to explode on the ground, which, for the time being, wasn't frozen. After a few minutes, he was able to walk back into the kitchen. He started to close the door behind him, but stopped. *I ought'a check on things at the main house. Let a faucet drip there, too.*

He hesitated, but a gust of icy wind convinced him he had to go there. Martha would have wanted that, would have insisted.

Chapter 8

He checked his pockets, then returned to the bedroom and removed his truck keys from the top of the washstand. After a moment's thought, he picked up the flashlight, went back to the kitchen door and poked his head out. The rain was slowing. Good.

Holding onto one of the posts supporting the porch roof, he went carefully down the slippery wood steps. In what seemed like only a second, he was in the cab of his truck. The wipers were sticky with the ice; they scrubbed across the windshield when he flipped the switch. He turned on the heater and pressed the gas pedal, racing the motor several minutes to make sure he wouldn't stall out.

Even with the weather, the quarter-mile drive was a short one, around the camp house onto the narrow lane where small treetops came together, forming a near-tunnel appearance until the lane reached a field he'd forgotten the name of. He drove up the lane, staring at the path ahead, watching the occasional slanted silver dashes in his headlights.

When he was feeling good, the farm was a beautiful place. When he was feeling bad, things were not so beautiful. But he never tired of the farm because the fields, woods and swamps were nearly as sweet as a friendship. There was never a change of heart about the way he felt about the farm. It was just when he didn't feel well, most things looked bad.

The winding lane was more of a path than a road. It went along the side of Gresham's Field to the acre-sized yard of the farmhouse.

Martha's family had left the farmhouse to her and Melvin. As far as anyone knew, it was her family's original house, and Melvin had worked to upgrade and modernize it from the year after they were married—the year Martha's parents turned it over to them and moved to Florida.

It was light-years in condition and appeal above the camp house. When Martha was still living, Melvin stayed at the main house all through the year except during hunting season, when he preferred the camp house for its proximity to the woods. Now, he preferred the camp house most of the time.

The house was rectangular, with eight five-foot columns on each side and a covered, open-air porch with a small widow's walk on top. The house had been added onto in the years before Martha's parents gave it to them. Now, it had three thousand, maybe thirty-five-hundred square feet. Melvin had never bothered to measure it, just knew it had ten rooms including two bathrooms. The ceilings were nine maybe ten feet, and the floors were all hardwood, with area rugs in the living room and two of the three bedrooms. The house's six fireplaces hadn't been used in twenty years. One of the rooms had been converted into a nursery. After Martha died, the nursery wasn't touched again.

The yard around the farm was always close-cut, and stayed green most of the year. Martha's flowerbeds were on both sides and in the back of the house. Melvin tended to the flowerbeds, and made sure they were always planted with fresh flowers in the spring. At first, it surprised him that he enjoyed working in the flowers. His favorite colors were deep yellows and blues with a sprinkle of red.

Melvin drove up the white gravel driveway that made a circle up to the front porch, passing in between the four large oaks and two wild hickory trees that lined its sides. To Melvin, the driveway looked like an inverted teardrop. Tonight, as the wind tore at them, the whipping tree limbs threw an ice-mist into his headlights.

Two ancient magnolia trees cuddled the northwest side of the house. Wisteria grew up one side of the front porch, providing a partial shield for the somewhat rusty porch swing. There was a small lean-to on the east side of the house. That's where he parked his truck.

A family of squirrels had made a home in the oaks and wild pecan trees around the structure. He nicknamed a few of the squirrels; there was Benny, Big Mama and Buster. He fed them peanuts and pecans on a weekly basis, and there was an unwritten agreement between them and Melvin: the animals could remain as long as they liked, provided they stayed out of the farmhouse.

A boar raccoon often stayed in an old shed near the house. Although wild, it seemed nearly tame when it came around, hungry and searching on the porch for food. Melvin named the raccoon Mr. Biggs.

Lady was an old doe who came into the yard with her fawns every evening in the spring. She would hang around until late summer, then leave and not return until the following spring. Melvin was always glad to see she'd made it through hunting season. He'd watched Lady for nearly six years, had seen her raise nine different fawns. Every now and again, other groups of deer came into the front yard, and even rested in the shade beneath the huge trees. But no one could get close to them. They were wild not as gentle-looking as Lady. This past spring, Lady didn't show up.

In the headlights, Melvin could see the gourds he'd strung up on a pole. Bluebirds made their homes in them. There was an old hickory tree by the well house, with a scar still visible in its trunk where Martha had sideswiped it while learning how to drive. A huge water oak still had a rope from which a tire swing had hung. The tree was a favorite tree of his, because he had fond memories of spinning Martha around and around in the tire until she screeched for him to stop.

Melvin was fussy about people going into the farmhouse without him knowing about it in advance. Didn't like it a bit. People around here knew it, and stayed away from his wrath. Only Chad could go in without notice. He always explained it wasn't that he didn't trust his friends and family. Any of them could go to the camp house without notice or permission. He just didn't want people coming in here when he wasn't around. And he didn't mind admitting how particular he was about his farmhouse, his yard and

Martha's flowerbeds.

This was always the hard part. The light rain reminded him of the evening Martha passed away. She'd sent word for him to come home while he was on a job. At five foot five inches, she'd gone from one hundred and twenty-five pounds to ninety pounds.

When they were dating, she told him if the weather permitted on Thanksgiving, they would place tables beneath the trees and invite a lot of people from church. That was a nice thing to do, Melvin had replied. Then she told him it was at a Thanksgiving dinner that she'd had her first kiss, from a fifteen-year-old boy from her church. It was something she'd never done, and she was shocked by it, and her eyes crinkled when she talked about it now. And Melvin's smile came back. After they married, they never had a church-dinner crowd at Thanksgiving, but at last, Melvin was able to stand to smell and eat a turkey again.

She loved sitting on that large front porch and staring across the fields slap down to Flat River. That evening, she could barely walk, and was angry that Melvin had to carry her to the porch. Then she asked him for a dipper of spring water. Not just a dipper; she wanted her fresh well water from a gourd. He fetched it for her and she drank deeply, and told him how good it tasted. And then they talked.

When she told him that when she went, he had to keep the farmhouse like it was, he promised her he would. Then she told him that he had to find sweetness and joy in his life after she was gone, even if it hurt. If he didn't, she'd haunt him and be angry. "Some folks just get unfortunate now and again," she had said. "I've been angry at God for a long time because we couldn't have kids. But I was wrong. God doesn't punish people like that. And don't you be angry, either. And when I get to heaven, some way or somehow, I'll send you a message or a sign."

He promised, and then opened his heart to her, told her how much she meant to him. At some point, she died in her rocking chair listening to him talk. He didn't even know she'd drifted off, just remembered how peaceful she looked. He buried her on the farm beneath a large willow tree so she could be in the shade. A place where she could see the fields and tree line to Flat River. Her headstone was right next to his.

He tried to find joy, just like he'd promised. It took him several years before he could look at another woman. He went out with several women that never measured up in his heart after being close to a woman like Martha. But he did find joy. On rare occasions, it brought tears to his eyes when he worked around her flowers, but just as soon as the tears came, they left. Working on her flowers and keeping the farmhouse in good condition was his gift, just like keeping the business going was his gift. She never wanted him to kill himself working, but for a long time after she passed, that's all he had.

Melvin got out of the truck, turned on his flashlight and shined the beam straight ahead as he walked across the grunting gravel up to the bottom step. The frigid gusts inhaled, exhaled and whirled through the tree limbs like the eerie noise in a conch shell while he retrieved the house key from its hiding place and unlocked the door.

As he walked down the hall, he glanced at Martha's picture, which sat on a small table stand. The eight-by-eleven black-and-white picture showed her leaning against a black 1945 Ford. The sleeves of her favorite white shirt were rolled up, and she had a wide smile. If the master bedroom door was open far enough in the mornings, the sun shone through it and warmed her picture.

He turned on the lights in the kitchen and looked around, then repeated the process in the other rooms, looking at each plaster ceiling to check for leaks. He never opened the door to the nursery. When he was finished, he walked back out the front door, locking it and putting the key back in its hiding place. He flipped the flashlight on and walked around the porch on both sides, turning the light toward the two sheds and A-frame barn diagonally behind the house. What he saw there made him pause.

* * *

Back in the truck, he drove toward the barn. His headlights traveled across the backyard to the quarter-acre garden that had been plowed up, readied for spring planting. What he'd seen were several big limbs that had fallen off the pecan trees. Other than that, things looked the same as the last time he'd checked it.

He took a swing around the barn and other

outbuildings, and shined the headlights on his three beehives, relieved the wind and rain hadn't damaged them. Satisfied, he drove back to the front of the farmhouse, down the gravel driveway and onto the path.

At the camp house, he went straight to the refrigerator, took down the note pad and wrote on it, then put the pad back on top of the refrigerator. In the bedroom, he returned the truck keys and flashlight to the top of the washstand. By the time he returned to the kitchen, the wind sounded feeble, the rain unhurried. If his instincts were right, the break in the weather was starting. His spirits lifted at the thought. He flipped the light switch on the back porch and went out, sucking in the cold air. When he exhaled, the fog curled and was rushed away by a draft of wind much gentler than before.

He removed a beer from the refrigerator, retrieved an opener from a drawer, and punched two holes in the can. After a long, long swallow, he returned to the table. He never understood why he felt the way he did when the weather was awful at night. There was something about daylight that made even the worst storm easier. In daylight, he could watch it rain. Weather wasn't a stranger in the daytime. Instead, he saw something magical and therapeutic that took him to a boundless place where he could breathe fresh and deep. *Who could have conceived rain, thunder, and lightning without knowing all?*

He sat in the soft, diffused light, letting his thoughts travel through the camp house across the fields, to the swamps, to the trees, to the barn, to the briar patches, to the trails, to Flat Creek . . . to the buck.

I bet that buck's making plans for me. Bet he's resting on the northwest side of a ravine. That's exactly where I'd be. Bet he's wondering where I'll hunt him tomorrow. My eyes and mind are young, just my age confines them. That's age for ya. Ruins a man's confidence. His strength, too.

He focused his thoughts on what he'd been fighting these past four years. An observer, someone just passing by, wouldn't see his inner turmoil at first. But it was there, just under the surface of his tired, pale-green eyes. No, they wouldn't see anything wrong until they saw his eyes staring blank off in the distance.

Enough is enough, he decided. *If I don't kill 'im. If another hunter don't get 'im before next year, I might have to kill 'im with my rifle. But only if I fail with the longbow this year.*

He couldn't bear thinking about his decision a moment longer, so he forced himself to refocus on the buck. *He's mad. Or maybe not. I wonder if a deer can even think. Yeah, I think this one probably can. Bet he thinks he's out-gamed me. He's sneaky. But I got a surprise: Yep, an old man and his longbow is gonna kill the largest whitetail buck ever seen. I'm gonna shoot that ole buck in his black heart with my flint arrowhead.*

Wonder if he ever gets tired of the hunt? Worry gives a man a half-life. Wonder if that buck ever worries, he doesn't seem to. It's as though he's waiting on me, just watching me, looking for me to make a mistake or do something stupid. Well, I'm not going to run away and hide from the bastard.

A small jolt of memory came to him; he'd forgotten to let the water drip at the main house. For a few minutes, he thought about going back, and then decided not to. It was too much trouble. Plus, the pipes were pretty deep under the house, out of the wind.

The cold and dark was thickening, and he wondered if he should leave the propane heater on when he did go to bed. *Best not to*, he decided. He knew from experience if he did, he'd have to get up later in the night and shut it off.

He stretched out his legs beneath the table, leaned back and extended his arms parallel to his shoulders, and yawned wide.

"Lordy," he said, and folded his arms on the table and stared with an inward gaze.

"I wonder if deer can sleep in weather like this?" he said aloud. Maybe if old Mossback didn't get a good night's sleep tonight, Melvin would have the advantage.

Just then he heard a thunderous pop, then something collapsed with a loud thump, shaking the ground and rattling windows. Wincing, he stood and went out on the back porch with his beer. *Had to be a big tree this time. And I believe I know exactly which tree it was.* If he was right, the big poplar at the end of the fencerow that separated the path from the road to the main farmhouse was no more.

The cold was deeper now, intruding through his clothes. He yawned again, wide and slow, and said quietly, "Oh, me." The action brought a cough, which led to several that sent a knifing pain beneath his left rib. He'd never felt a pain like it, and wondered if it was a pulled muscle. But it went away as soon as he stopped coughing. *Nothing to worry about. Just a side-stitch.*

He poured out what was left of his beer, more foam than liquid now, and crumpled the can with his right hand before wandering back into the cabin. Looking around the room, he began to quarrel with himself about going to bed. That's when the sky detonated and the windows shook almost instantly thereafter. When he breathed in, the smell was a thin string of sour sweat, urine, gunpowder, rotting flesh, and familiar cuss-words.

Now, in this slowing of time, an unnatural sense that mud, sweat and blood were on his face drove a slithering chill to his core. He remained motionless, grimly staring at the battlefield near Breuvannes, France, dragged back to July 28, 1918 near the Ourcq River. He felt the wisp of a bullet so close to his head, he felt its heat on the end of his tongue.

He didn't try to push back the recollection. It, together with the wind and rain, whisked away his burden of trying to stay awake.

He had no regrets about his wartime experiences or his memories of them, but they were growing fuzzier. He believed now it was better to be armed with good sense than armed with a gun of war. Yet to him, men who served in the armed forces were noble, brave and honest. Veterans had a special camaraderie, a bond that cures with age. The comradeship he felt was more than giving your last drink of water to another soldier in need. It was on a higher plane. Most don't understand if they never served. He always had a soft heart for another veteran.

I should keep my mouth shut about Chad going into the military, he thought, and walked into his bedroom, stooped down and slid a cardboard box out from beneath his cot. He carried it into the kitchen and rested it on the table. The box was sealed with duct tape. He removed the tape and opened the flaps.

Inside the box was rabbit tobacco, pine needles and leaves over a set of camouflage clothing: his hunting clothes. The rabbit tobacco, together with pine needles, moss and small chunks of swamp mud permeated the clothing. That was intentional.

A deer's nose is keen, but he believed deer weren't alarmed by the odor of a human except when hunting season was nearing. He'd often witnessed that; when hunting season was out, the deer weren't alarmed or as wild as they were during the season. Deer have a second sense about things, he had learned. The clothing gave him confidence that a deer would smell only what was natural in the environment, and not human odors.

He walked over to the set of deer antlers nailed into the wall and removed his lucky hat, a floppy-brimmed camouflage hat that once looked like an Australian outback hat. After it was washed, the brim softened and drooped. The perfect hat for bow hunting.

He knew from experience that the wrong hat could corrupt a hunter's draw, so he was careful about the type and kind of hat he wore. Sometimes he wouldn't wear a hat at all. Other times, he'd just use the hat to dust himself off before going out hunting, hoping the hat would leave a dust-charm of good luck.

He put the hat in the box, folded the top and returned the box beneath his cot, then pulled open the top drawer of the washstand. He lifted up some clothing, counting the number of clean cotton socks he had. He counted five pairs—more than enough right now. He closed the drawer. His inner clock told him it was finally time to go to bed.

Preparation for the hunt was as routine as his off-season life, and never varied. He started by laying out his hunting gear in a specific order, so he wouldn't waste time when he got up. He checked his arrow and longbow again, then everything from his razor-sharp knife to the bowstring. The clothes he'd wear went on the adjacent bunk. To them he added a six-foot-long nylon cord, folded and tied together with a rubber band, toilet paper, gloves and the flashlight. He removed his trousers and shirt, pulled on his insulated long johns, then placed a blue toboggan cap on his balding head. After turning off the light, he slid into his sleeping bag and zipped it up.

He listened to the rain, to the popping tin, to the plastic rattling and to water dripping and splashing. He closed his eyes and went over the path he might take to the hunting area. He thought about the rooster he'd been hearing for years, and wondered if he'd hear that rooster crow in the morning.

Time slowed, and he drifted into a gray and dark realm. Dreaming, he saw ashen trees swaying against a dark sky, and a field he'd never seen before, grown up in large plants he couldn't identify. Then he was an Indian stalking with his longbow in a forest of enormous cypress trees laden in silk, a place where diamonds dangled from the leathery green leaves of enormous oaks. There was no sun, just a sky of yellow gold illuminating wild foxes, wolves, coyotes, raccoons, ducks, turkeys, blue jays, and deer with eyes that looked like sparkling white whirlwinds. They were familiar and the sight made him happy.

At a distance, he could see a dog on a grassy knoll together with another image: a wide slough with cold black water that gave no reflections. The sight frightened him, because the slough separated him from both the dog and the odd shape next to it. A wide log lay across the slough, but, with each step he took, the log became narrower and narrower. Afraid to continue, he rushed back to the other side. He decided to search for another log to cross. He heard a rooster crow and awakened, but tried to get back to his dream.

In the twilight of sleep, he could hear the window-plastic rattling and the splashing rain. Again time slowed, and he returned to the dream where he was an Indian stalking with his longbow. A rumbling sounded, and he didn't want to stop dreaming, but the distant noise wouldn't let him rest.

He rolled over and looked at the florescent arms of the clock. 4:43 a.m. He closed his eyes and lay in his sleeping bag listening, thinking about the weather and the direction he'd take into the swamps—and about the Indian stalking the buck.

Chapter 9

He sat up in the cot, leaned over and flipped the light switch on, and yawned wide. He could have taken advantage of the weather and slept later, but he couldn't miss daylight's arrival on any day. He loved the sob-songs of morning, especially on the morning of a hunt.

After a few moments, he pulled on his camp-house clothes and went outside on the porch, then into the bathroom to empty his bladder. He was met by the tooth-jarring freeze that had arrived behind the storm.

When he was back on the porch and exhaled, his breath changed into a frosty haze. The cold pressed against his clothing like a police pat-down. All that remained of the once-powerful wind were ice-covered tree limbs on the ground. The rain was another matter: In the thinning dark, tree trunks, shrubbery were taking shape. Thin silver dashes, old and slowing down, seemed to float in the porch light's glow.

He looked up and saw the moon's bright halo breaching through the lessening clouds. This was a good sign. He went back in the camp house and closed the door behind him.

The house was silent except for the occasional popping tin, or when the floor squeaked. He knelt and held a match to the heater's eye. Yellow, blue, crimson and orange flames went linear, then leaped with a roar like fans at a football game. As he knew he would, he felt young, unbeatable.

The filled kettle went onto the stove, and he sat at the table and thought about breakfast.

It's too early for bacon and eggs. If I eat this early, I'll be hungry by mid-afternoon. It's hard to remain motionless if you're cold and hungry. Hunger pangs made him nervous and anxious, especially if he was hunting. He believed it would have been simpler for nature to compromise between old men and their requirement for food. *After all, nature compromised with old men and their other wants. Why not food? Maybe old men might be more pleasant if they didn't have hunger pains.*

Early morning coffee was a compromise, he thought. *If inspiration strikes after the first cup, so much the better.*

He never drank coffee until his early thirties, and then only because Martha drank it. Those were the good times, when he learned how much the aroma of hot, perked coffee in the morning brightened up a day. When he lost her, he stopped perking coffee in the morning and switched to instant. It didn't help much. The aroma always reminded him of her.

The water in the kettle was boiling. He made a cup of coffee, then took a long, careful slurp before peeking out the window. White frost and ice that pressed against the windowpanes was already changing into minuscule, clear, winding creeks. Daylight was coming fast.

It would be several hours before he could settle on

what the weather was going to do, and he thought about going back to sleep for an hour. Once up though, that was a tough thing to do. There was something magical about being up and stirring before daylight anyway.

But, sleeping or not, he did need to hang around until he figured out the weather. If it turned for the better, he'd hunt the oak ridge instead of the island. The oak ridge attracted lots of game because of the abundance and variety of food. A bit too open for a cagey old buck with any self-respect to travel in daylight, but an easy place to get to, and to hunt. A convenience-seeking hunter would probably go there first. It was something to think about anyway.

Maybe that's it, he thought, his realization almost causing the cup to slip out of his hand. *He knows my habits like I know many of his habits. Don't believe anything would expect me on the island today. If I were him, I'd stay put there and try to catch me after dark-thirty, walking out when I can't see so well. I know that's what he'd like to do!*

After he finished the coffee, Melvin went out and walked to the edge of the porch. By leaning against the rail, he could look up and see gray, thinning clouds floating east. When he dropped his gaze to eyelevel, he could see the tree limbs taking shape. As he peered into the woods, he heard a wood thrasher's song against the roar of a jet passing high overhead.

Across the lane, tree limbs were encased in ice and were stressed. But the wind was dying and that was good;

human odor wouldn't float and spread out low to the ground, alarming the game. He believed human odor would rise because of a man's heat. But when it rained, human scent didn't travel a great distance, probably was soaked along with everything else in the swamps.

After a few moments, he went back into the camp house to his bedroom, found a light camouflage jacket and put it on. He returned to the kitchen and sat down to listen for a while longer. The sunlight was visible now, and he was glad. He managed to bear it, but he hated the cold. If the sun made it out, it would warm things up. "Once weather makes up its mind to leave," he said aloud, "deer make up their mind to feed." The truth in that made him smile.

Years of experience had taught him much about the weather and how deer responded to it. It seemed to him that deer moved around better right after a rain. And, he believed, deer were generally miserable in a downpour. A buck, especially, was nervous when it poured, because the rain confused sounds, and the buck became edgy because its senses were dulled. He'd seen bucks in briar patches with their antlers sticking up, never hearing him slipping up on them in the rain. On more than one occasion he'd hunted in the rain, stalking around briar patches and in the thick underbrush.

Any good hunter would take a chance on any day, regardless of the weather, to bag a buck. Weather was important, but it was better to be in the woods despite the weather conditions. That's what separated the true hunter from the average hunter. You can't kill a buck if you're around the camp at lunch, or because it's raining: something an inexperienced hunter might never appreciate or understand. That's why, when Melvin hunted the big buck, he remained all day in the swamps, returning only at dark.

He glanced at the window, but the weather's direction refused to reveal itself to him.

After an endless couple of hours thinking about what to do and waiting for the weather to show its hand, he took a nap. When he woke, the wind had worn out and the gray clouds had moved east, presenting a blue sky. A bold noon sun turned the ice to drips. On the porch, he had to shield his eyes from the glare. After all, it had been nearly five days since he'd seen the sun. The cold remained, though. When he exhaled, the air boiled into clouds before it vanished.

It's time, he thought. *I want to be comfortable in the ground stand before the deer start to feed.*

He'd decided to hunt the buck from the ground stand he'd made years ago, next to the water oak tree on the seventy-five-acre island. The tree near where he'd found the flint arrowhead. The well-camouflaged stand was in an ideal location to fake out a deer. The area had sapling thickets, and swamp briars that would shred clothes and flesh off a man if he ran through them. The water oak tree was a prized place for squirrels, too. He couldn't remember a single year when that big oak wasn't fruitful.

Not long ago, he could stand on the camp house's back porch and see clear across the open field down to the oak ridge. The rows in the open field were straight, the prettiest rows . . . *heck, the finest field on the farm*. The rich, dark dirt could grow anything. He remembered how tall the corn grew, the cotton, millet, soybeans, peanuts and hay. The barbeques, the dove shoots, the quail-hunting parties, all gone now. A once proud and mighty field consumed by rugged sapling trees and thick briars. The growth provided a refuge for game now, and that was all.

"I wished I hadn't let the field get in this condition," he whispered, his voice turned to gravel. "If I was younger, I'd push down every tree, every broom sage and clear out all the growth and burn it. But Chad will get it cleaned up. I'll see the rows grow again in this field."

Because it was surrounded by swamps, Melvin was about the only person who hunted the island. Chad would, but he never went to the area of the island alone, just with Melvin. Melvin understood.

If there were any spooky swamps on the planet, they were right there, surrounding the island, which nearly always had a light fog that would hang around longer than any other fog Melvin had seen. The fog might have been ancient spirits. Melvin grinned. If they *were* ancient spirits, they must like old hunters.

Melvin knew where every tree was, every game trail, where every otter slide was located on the slough. Yet even he didn't feel comfortable on the island when it was dark, or about to be. Partly, he supposed, it was because he sensed the buck stalking him. Or maybe it was because the only way to access the island was the old fallen log that was often underwater after a very hard rain.

"I can't imagine the water reaching its peak before midnight tonight," he muttered. "By that time, I should be out of the swamps."

He made one scrambled egg and bacon for lunch, then went into his narrow bedroom and pulled on his insulated long johns. A heavy sweatshirt was next, then the camouflage coveralls, cotton socks, and knee-high rubber boots.

He decided to take an extra pair of socks, and change into them when he got to the stand. "My feet will sweat and freeze if I don't," he muttered, then smiled. "Those gloves Chad bought me ought to come in handy today."

He walked to the wall where his bow quiver hung. *Ought not to take it today*, he mused. *Too cold and wet outside. It might freeze and get brittle . . . But what the hell.* His alternative—going back to the farmhouse to get the rifle—wasn't for this year, but next year.

He took down the flint arrow and the quiver, allowing a moment to admire the hawk's tail feather. Besides being a good luck charm, the tail feather was his wind-direction finder. "Hope you *do* bring me luck," he mumbled, "'cause, mercy, it's cold today."

He removed the floppy camouflage hat from the box

beneath his cot and placed it on his head. "Better leave the porch light on," he said aloud. After he flipped the switch, he turned the heater off.

Outside, he took the longbow and pulled the string back with his three fingers several times. The limbs moaned. He nocked the arrow into the string and pulled it back again. Satisfied, he took the arrow and put it into the quiver, shrugged it over his shoulder, then checked to make sure he had his knife, cord, extra socks and gloves, flashlight and matches. He leaned the bow against the wall to close the door.

Bow in hand; he walked across the porch and down the steps. The sun bore down causing him to squint as he started down the path. The path went along the oak ridge to the spot he used to go to the island. He couldn't see the oak ridge now, but he knew every tree, every bend on the way there.

Ice glistened and dripped off branches. The trees didn't roll back and forth and the limbs didn't sway. Just as he predicted, the wind was gone.

CHAPTER 10

From a distance, even those who knew him well might not have recognized him. There was something about the way he walked. You could see it in his stride, his battle dress, in the way he held his longbow, the way he looked off in the distance. The way his floppy hat fit, the way the hawk's tail feather floated behind him. He stopped when he reached the end of the lane. A small footpath squeezed and intersected the lane there.

After reaching back and pulling the flint arrow from his bow quiver, he nocked it onto the bowstring, then slowed his pace and crouched, watching for action and listening to sounds. An observer might have called it an impromptu practice session, but it really wasn't. He always crouched when he crept along.

The swamps and moss-covered trees were bright and inviting, and the thought of his ground stand being in an ideal spot encouraged him.

He was in no rush, and avoided unnecessary sounds as he eased along. His floppy camouflage hat provided a convenient shade for his eyes. He watched the shadows.

He stopped and looked around steadily for a few moments, then un-nocked the arrow and put it in the quiver. He leaned the bow against a tree. Raising his right boot above his left knee, he used a stick to rake off the mud that had accumulated on his boot, and did the same to the other boot. When that was done, he removed the arrow from his quiver and nocked it on the string again.

Remaining motionless, he gazed steadily through the trees at the wonderland of vines and briars, a few old stumps, a weathered wood fencepost, a game trail, a discarded beer can and a gum wrapper, a concrete block, a faded red ribbon tied to a limb, the rusty fender of an old car, and the old rock chimney standing alone in the shade of the trees. Here, the sun beams were weak, and each object was still covered in a layer of ice.

Only after he verified there was no movement ahead of him did he slip as cautious as a predator into the woods. His reactions were slower, yet his ears remained as fine-tuned as an animal.

He knew the voice of each violin, each reed, each horn, each drum and each cymbal produced by the swamps. Even a bird, a squirrel darting away was observed or listened to with keen interest. Each sound added up.

Even his movements were intended to deceive curious eyes. He remained in the shade as much as he could when he crept along the trail. He'd pick out an ice-glazed tree trunk, go to it and remain hidden, looking, searching with his eyes until he moved again.

It probably didn't mean anything to most, but to him it was the stalking method of a hunter, a method developed by animals over ages as they zeroed in on their prey, slipping up on them when they least expected it. Other times, he'd squat and look across the surface of the ground, searching for legs, a snout, part of an antler, anything white, or perhaps one brown eye peering at him from behind a tree.

It was a challenge to see who could see the other first: the deer or the man. He knew if he saw the deer before the deer saw him, the deer might not ever see him. *And vice versa*, he thought, allowing his lips to curl into a smile.

Constantly prepared for the unexpected, he investigated every tree trunk five feet above the ground, then down to the ground before he got to it. He used all his senses. Even the most distant sounds were listened to as if he were eavesdropping on a conversation. A buck would let you walk on by if it felt secure and confident that you didn't see it. But he wasn't after just any buck.

It was going to be a long afternoon in his ground stand. He would try to stay until a minute before dark—the latest he could stay and feel truly safe on the island.

He might not make it that long; it was colder than he could remember, and he wasn't sure if he could hold out. He'd worry about it later, though. A true hunter would go back to the camp only after he gave the hunt his best efforts.

He knew, once a deer fed, its only purpose was to bury itself in cover until dark. At dark, the deer moved in great numbers and travel miles before returning to their hideouts. Deer would be feeding early today, and he was sure of it.

He wanted to catch the big buck when it least expected it.

He'd walk fifty or sixty feet, then stop and look around, observing carefully everything he saw by moving his eyes right, then left, looking close to the ground. Then he'd slowly turn his head, following the same 180-degree half-circle. Other times he would stop, turn around, and look along the path he just traveled, listening.

It's nearly impossible to spot a deer standing motionless fifty yards through the brush and trees, he thought, *but I've seen 'em before, and will again.* His sixty-eight-year-old memory might fail him from time to time, but his eyes and ears were as good as ever.

The bright sun shining on the trees made the limbs look like they'd had a polished. He couldn't look in the direction of the two o'clock sun, so he remained in the cold shadows like his eyes remained in the shade made by the brim of the floppy hat.

The ageless instinct to kill was ever-present in him. When he first deer hunted he killed for food. After, he killed for numbers and for ego. Then he hunted only the big bucks; they presented more of a challenge. No matter his reason, he never wasted a deer or killed wantonly. If he couldn't use the meat, he'd give it to family or friends who were grateful to have the meat.

As he traveled along the path, he listened to the birds because they gave signals about animal movements. Birds chanted out an alarm if disturbed. A brown wood thrasher would always let him know when something was near. The thrasher huddled close to the ground and darted from danger while making a muted coughing sound.

He heard a rustle or was it water dripping from limbs. Something made a noise.

He stopped.

He searched the area with his senses. As he listened, the faint, churning roar of water spilling over the beaver dam came to him.

He looked down at the ground in front of him. When he saw where several deer had moved along the ridge, he decided to stop and wait a few minutes.

Then he spotted an enormous rub on a small sapling. He quietly crept closer and saw that the scrape on the tree was as high as his shoulder. An enormous buck had made the rub with its antlers.

Just as he returned to the trail, he saw something dart across, too fast for him to see it. He crept over to a low-hanging limb. Beneath the limb, fresh dirt was exposed in a rectangular. A fresh paw place of about two foot made right after the storm. *The bucks are moving,* he thought. *About two hours old. It's early for rutting season, but . . . this buck's in a hurry to find a doe must be a young buck.*

When a doe found the paw-place, she would urinate in the cleared spot, then leave. When the buck returned, he would follow the scent no matter where the doe traveled. At times of rutting, a buck became careless and ignored danger. He had one thing in his mind: finding the doe that left her scent. Many times, a buck had to fight another buck to gain access to the doe that left the scent trail.

Seeing the paw-place on the ground made him believe bucks were starting to rut now, rather than around Christmas, probably because of the unseasonably winter weather. The timing of truly cold weather played an important role in a buck's rut in the Deep South, he believed. And it was cold now.

With even greater resolve to be quiet, Melvin went forward, listening to the water with such intent, he barely heard the housedog barking in the distance. The old man's fingers didn't throb. So far, the cold wasn't getting to him.

He'd gone thirty yards when he looked to his left and saw the doe. She was standing still, staring at the old man curiously. After a moment, when some nearby blue jays started bickering, she twisted her ear to the left, lowered her head, and then raised it to return her gaze to his. Then she stomped her front hooves on the ground, turned and leaped ten yards, and stopped. Her long, fluffy white flag of a tail looked like a wedding veil.

The doe looked over her front shoulders and glared at him, then snorted several times, warning all within hearing that danger was near. Two more bounces, and she vanished into the piney thicket. He stood frozen, watching, listening, pleased that his intuitions about the weather and deer were correct.

Stealth and motionlessness are a hunter's friends, he thought. He knew a doe would take the lead in a danger area and lead out a buck, going about fifty or a hundred yards ahead of the buck like a point man on a combat patrol. Her purpose in doing so was similar: to search the avenue she was traveling to detect danger. She would give out an alarm by making blowing sounds, warning the buck to run back in the direction he'd just traveled. At other times, Melvin had seen an older buck use a younger, immature buck to lead. The older buck would remain seventy-five or a hundred yards behind the younger buck. If an inexperienced deer hunter were in the avenue of approach the young buck was traveling, the inexperienced hunter would take the young buck, and the hunter would never know a much larger buck was following nearby.

This was only one of the methods deer used to avoid detection. Using scent, sight, hearing and camouflage to their advantage, man never really had a chance once a deer spotted them. Deer are as stealthy as a highly trained sniper, their bodies made for deception. A deer coming straight at you is no wider than four to eight inches; a small tree trunk can hide their body. Once, he'd walked within ten yards of a buck standing still, and never saw it until his peripheral vision caught a glimpse of the buck twitching an ear. That buck was standing near its paw-place.

* * *

When Melvin arrived at the slope on the ridge, he looked down at the bottom, which was full of muddy water from the previous night's rain. The once-calm water was growing strong; it lapped at the bottom of the foot log fifty yards away, and foam swirled around it. The foot log, once a mammoth oak tree, was at least five feet in diameter before it fell across the narrowest part of the slough. For the past twenty years, it had made the perfect footbridge. Even if the water kept rising, it was unlikely the foot log would dislodge.

He looked across the flat and saw water spilling out in places around the slough, encroaching on the flats where his ground stand was located. The slough was twenty feet wide at the foot log, but wider in other places around the bank. He'd never seen the slough without water. Even in drought years, the slough always had water.

"Don't think I've ever seen the water *that* high, though," he whispered, looking down at the enormous oak near where his stand was located. The ground stand wasn't yet visible, but no doubt, it was still there. No doubt the coyotes were still on the island too.

Narrow Gap Slough circled the island and provided water to the wildlife that lived on it: wood ducks, mallards, beaver, otter, small bream, snapping turtles and raccoons. There were plenty of places to hide, and plenty of food for them. Also the favorite place of a tribe of coyotes. Few wolves were in the area.

Nevertheless, wolves in small killer packs did travel through the swamps in early spring. It was unusual to see a wolf, but he knew when they were around; he could hear them at night. They'd duel with the coyotes, yelping and yodeling at the moon. But as far as he knew, the yodeling contest was as far as their competition went. When the wolves came through the swamps in early spring, they minded their own business, and the coyotes liked it that way.

There was something spooky about the island today. It had a mysterious look, something out of a ghost book even now, in the direct sun. The oak ridge circled it like a huge meteor crater, steep in some places and gently rolled in other spots. He called that ridge The Rim. It went for miles before circling back around.

He couldn't remember who told him, but someone said that Creek Indians felt the swamps held spirits of their ancestors: spirits that dwelled there and hunted on certain nights. On cool, chilly nights, when the full moon was bright, you could hear sounds from the swamps that made you wonder if the Creek Indians weren't right.

After removing the arrow and placing it into his bow quiver, Melvin used a sapling as a walking stick to carefully maneuver the slope, grasping trees from time to time to steady him as he traveled down. On his quiver, the hawk's tail feather rocked to one side, then the other as he moved carefully down the ridge.

When he got to the foot log, he paused and gave a low whistle of surprise. He gauged the water to be about seven or eight feet deep—higher than he'd seen it in years. Placing one foot carefully after the other, he walked across the worn log. When he reached the other side, he leaned the longbow against the trunk, removed his thick gloves and blew into his praying hands. Then he urinated in the water.

When his gloves were once more snug against his fingers, he looked down at the swamp floor. Brown, matted leaves and indentations in the mud told him a few deer had traveled here earlier. He saw what looked like several dog tracks, too, but they were coyote tracks.

He looked in the direction of his ground stand, removed the arrow and nocked it. Then, he crept forward.

His stand had been built, rebuilt and moved over the course of four years. Now, it was positioned near a small thicket of briars and saplings beneath a large oak. The saplings always struggled for sunlight. Like them, his ground stand adapted to its environment, and was well camouflaged to look like an almost waist-high circle of brush around the small, two-foot-diameter oak tree.

He'd used material readily available in the swamp to build it, mostly fallen limbs, moss, and mud from the slough to cement it together. He believed deer knew the difference between when hunting season was near, and when hunting season was in.

The mud and moss came together to conceal his absence or presence inside the stand. This combination, he believed, also cut down on an animal's ability to detect motions made by his hands, or small movements his body might make instinctively. Mud, moss, branches and leaves were a technique he'd used for years to conceal his scent.

When he built the stand, he took some swamp briars and tied them to branches, with small logs along the side. Then he put moss around the exterior perimeter, lots of moss on the interior ground, too, along with rabbit tobacco he found in the fields of broom sage. He'd used moss and rabbit tobacco for years, liked using it because their scent and appearance were familiar to deer.

The outside of the stand he left pretty much alone, but he kept the ground on the interior clean of mud and leaves with the moss he'd taken from trees. He put moss around his neck, and sometimes on top of his head to shield his face. By doing so, investigating eyes were betrayed, fooled.

Other times, if he was on an all-day hunt, he'd lie down on the soft moss and take a catnap. Except during the summer months. Then, he removed all the moss, and lie down on the warm earth.

Copperheads liked to hide beneath moss. He had a six-gallon bucket he'd painted coffee brown and pale green. The bucket was just the right height for him to sit on so he could peer over the top edge of the stand.

He crept to the stand like a predator; he walked crouched, watching as he eased along the narrow, worn-out path, instinct telling him where to place his boots with each step. The stand's half-height gate, made of moss and limbs, opened without sound. He always looked inside the stand before he entered. Occasionally, snakes and other animals were in there, seeking refuge from bad weather. But there was no threat of snakes now, because it was too cold. Today, it was empty.

He removed the arrow from the bow and went inside, then leaned the bow and quiver against the stand's frame within easy reach. A quick inspection told him the knapsack was still there.

Kept in the stand year-round, he had coated it with mud and rabbit tobacco. Its contents, which rarely varied, were surrounded by plastic to protect them. Inside were canned beans and wieners, tins of sardines, packs of crackers, two canned Cokes, plastic spoons and forks, napkins, matches, a six-foot nylon cord, a small flashlight and a paperback book of Civil War poems, among other small items.

Melvin lowered himself to the bucket and lifted the knapsack onto his lap. When he opened it, he frowned; the two Cokes had frozen, their seams had burst. He removed them and leaned them up against the frame of the stand, reminding himself to take them with him when he left.

The other items seemed all right, so he closed the knapsack and placed it back in its original spot, then leaned his back against the trunk of the oak and folded his arms. The sun to his back, he looked out across the flats.

He felt the need to cough, but didn't want any animals nearby to hear him, so he tucked his chin into the top of his camouflage coveralls.

When he coughed, the faint, knifelike pain under his left arm made him wince. The cough was muted, but to him it was loud, and he cursed inwardly. *I'm making too much noise. Might as well just jump up and yell, I'm here, avoid the area!" Might as well go back to the camp house.*

But, of course, he stayed. He took a deep, careful breath and the pain didn't come back, so he sat straight up on the bucket until only his head appeared above the rim of the stand and watched.

His eyes like slits, for any kind of movement. The cold was beginning to sink to his flesh, and his toes began to ache. He thought about the dry socks he'd brought, but decided to wait. Between settling in and the cough, he'd already put half the island on alert. To take his mind off the tinge of pain in his chest, he allowed his mind to shift inward.

Chapter 11

If God ever made a quiet place to relax, this is the place, he thought. *But sometimes too quiet. Like today.* A crisp, cool day was the best day to hunt. A wet, soggy day with bright sun like this was a marginal second best. He couldn't hear a deer walk in a distance.

But then again, they might not hear *him* as well, either. After a while, a quick glance at his boots caused him to reach out for a small stick, which he used to rake the mud off them.

His movements were cautious and deliberate; if a deer was watching, all it took was one movement and it made difference if it was a big or small movement. Deer are curious, but only the youngest, most inexperienced deer would investigate movements during hunting season.

He gently returned the stick to the ground and leaned back, gratified at the silence. *Everything's so still when I first get here. Like everything's holding its breath waiting for me to make a move, or for the buck to make a move. Like other animals know I'm here hunting for the buck.* His face hardened at the thought, and he shifted his toes inside his boots to wake them up.

These swamps seem gentle to an innocent eye, but I know better. In spite of that, I'd still rather be here than be on the interstate driving to a job every day, or in town with the other old men, or watching television or reading a book.

Those who prefer the company of others can never understand or really see what a magnificent place this is. That's why they disapprove. Or maybe they're right. Maybe I am an old fool for being out in this weather.

Knowing better, he smiled at that. *The buck's won the first rounds, but now it's in the late rounds. Maybe I'll get lucky today.*

Melvin peered in the direction of a particular gray-brown and black thicket. The thicket kept direct wind away, and the big oak tree sheltering it kept much of the direct rain off the thicket. It was used by all kinds of game, but Melvin had found signs that the buck hid there, too.

The longer he waited, the more his senses attuned to the environment. Now, he heard distant sounds that weren't flooded out by the rushing water, like the familiar wailing of a Lord God. Woodsmen gave the name Lord God to this particularly big species of redheaded woodpecker: the kind of name you'd say if you heard it above you, pecking away on a big hollow tree, while you were alone in the swamps.

Melvin knew exactly what it was; so did other animals, who were never afraid of the panicked, knocking noise it made.

Yet those same animals run and hide when they hear a tiny noise made by dry leaves when I slip along, he thought, snuffling to quell his urge to laugh at the irony. A small limb breaking was enough to scatter all animals within hearing distance.

Can't blame 'em, he thought. *An animal knows another animal won't intentionally break a limb on the ground—unless it's running away. So they know the noise is usually because of a human.*

The thought made Melvin's heart seize up a bit. To others, he insisted his only age-related change was his memory. But there was more. His ability to ease along quietly was becoming more forced each year. He found it difficult to squat in order to go beneath a limb or overhanging tree trunk. He used to go right beneath them without any lost motion, and almost no sound. Now, he tended to walk around them or find another route.

The sun was now at the top of the trees on the oak ridge, lighting up the swamp bottoms and casting shadows on the dark, soaked leaves around him. Soon it would begin sinking farther. He figured he had at least three hours maybe more of daylight to hunt.

The sun was over his left shoulder and, while he felt its warmth on his shoulders, he wasn't warm. His toes were starting to ache more. He should stretch out his legs to get better circulation them. Or change socks. *Or maybe I might as well go back to the camp house and let the buck win another round.*

That thought, and any of discomfort, was pushed back, way back, and his eyes returned to slits as he watched the scene around him.

Twenty minutes had gone when he heard the familiar

whistling sounds made by wood ducks. Then he saw arched wings tilt, rock side to side and pivot, then come down through the tree limbs like a fast-moving football splashing on the surface of the rushing water not far from him.

Wood duck drakes are handsome ducks, he thought. *Those arched wings are like Cupid's bow.* Wood ducks were fragile and easy to knock down, though. Melvin would rather eat a wood duck, but he preferred to shoot a mallard.

In the distance a squirrel squawked, then another one somewhere along the slough picked up its warning. Melvin knew squirrels barked at anything, and ignored their noise.

But when he saw an owl swoop down, then rest on the huge limb of a white oak tree, he looked across the flats and watched black-gray vines curve, bend, then drop down from the trees. The oak trees' sparse green leaves and a few gold leaves swayed back and forth, but nothing else. In the distance, he could hear a group of blue jays getting loud and rowdy. He smiled. *When blue jays group, they act like juvenile delinquents.*

A jet passed over; he looked up and saw a thin white straight line buried deep in the sky. *I wonder what everything looks like from that altitude. Wonder what the back of clouds look like from that high up.* But he didn't want his thoughts to meander there. Instead, he closed his eyes and listened to the swamps. Sounds he knew well.

After a while, he opened his eyes and looked back toward the slough. The water and foam reminded him of an ice cream float sprinkled with cinnamon growing into islands as they pushed against the tree trunks, like rapids in the cinnamon-hued water. The sight reminded him of his trip down the Colorado River through the Grand Canyon. The Colorado River was a mean and dangerous river. His boat was nearly destroyed on several rapids. *The Grand Canyon is where the earth's soul quarrels with itself. I don't want to ride on the earth's soul again. That one time was enough.*

He fixed his gaze on the oak and its enormous limbs that stretched out from the tree's trunk. The limbs were loaded with moss. He'd measured the oak twelve years ago, and it was eighteen feet across the base. He watched a big cat squirrel searching for acorns beneath the giant tree. It looked bored as it fed, and appeared to be choosing only the best acorns. His eyes rested again on the thicket where he was sure his trophy relaxed, slept, and challenged him. He knew if that buck came out, he'd let him know who the winner was.

Ole buck, I bet you're still wet and cold. Not comfortable like I am right now. Why not end this hunt and come out of your hiding place? Just walk out and turn broadside, and I'll sink this flint arrowhead deep into your shoulder. You probably won't feel a thing. Just like a sharp blow from a fist. I can't live forever, and neither can you. And that'll end it for us both.

You're too cagey for that, aren't you? As calculating as a poker player. I wish we could talk. You could tell me 'bout times you had me, and I could tell you 'bout times I thought

I had you. We've got a lot in common, I bet. You love this island, and so do I. You're probably seven to nine years old—a long time in buck-years—and feel like half the buck you were before. Kind 'a like me, too.

He threw out a last challenge, one he'd made many times in the past four years. *I'm betting you can't stay put today. I have a hunch you'll move around. Yeah, you will. You're watching me just like I'm watching you.*

The challenge formally given, he leaned his head back against the tree trunk and looked up. Naked limbs and tiny twigs bent, twisted and stretched, reaching up to touch the sky. Those sights reminded him of the back of his hands, veined and speckled and beginning to wither with age.

He closed his eyes and listened, thought about how cold he was. The tips of his toes still ached, and his fingers were starting to numb. He made a fist and placed the ball between his legs. He should change socks to keep his toes from freezing, but he made no move to do so, just listened to the water and wondered how rapidly it was encroaching onto the flats. *There's no way anyone's going to travel on Fannie Road to get in here tonight. Water's probably over Flat Creek Bridge by now. Wonder if Chad will try to make it here this evening if he returns from Pensacola. Bet that wife of his will keep him in Pensacola tonight.* Melvin tried, but at that moment, he couldn't remember her name.

There was no sound, no perceived motion as the catalyst, but he opened his eyes and looked back at the thicket. He watched it a few moments, never moving his head. Something was out of place. He squinted; saw it. A big black shape was moving slowly, and then it would stop. As he watched, the image eased from his sight.

He watched the vacant spot a moment more, then slipped his hand to his longbow and bought it back to his lap. He slipped the glove from his right hand, slowly removed the flint arrow from the quiver and nocked it in the string, noting that his frozen fingers could barely feel it, or even his movements.

Just my luck.

The bow resting on his lap, he blew air into his cupped hands to warm them enough to get a better grasp.

Just as he lifted his head to the small opening he'd made in the thicket, he saw a huge turkey, then another, walk into the clearing. He wanted to laugh. He'd had many, many chances to kill an old gobbler with his bow. He watched the turkeys until they waddled out of his sight.

He saw several wood ducks in the distance, circling in the sky, and watched as they arched and rocked their wings, then came down through the limbs with a whoosh. *It's amazing how ducks can dive in so fast and not hit a tree limb and get killed*, he thought in appreciation. *When they land on the water, it's almost like they splatter. They're so beautiful, so fragile.*

He pulled on the glove and folded his arms, putting his gloved hands beneath his armpits, then rested the back of his head against the tree trunk and closed his eyes.

Smells so fresh and clean here. The sun on my shoulder makes everything right. Just wish it would do the same for my hands and feet.

He would have been content just to sit there, but feared the cold was about to chase him out. He'd just moved his foot to start to stand when his body froze. He wasn't yet sure where the noise came from, but he knew it was the sound of bucks fighting. The sounds of clashing antlers were clear. Then the world went silent.

When it came again, he recognized that the duel was occurring on top of the oak ridge. He slowly shifted his body to his left and looked back toward the top of the ridge, remaining at that angle until he was confident the match was over. He waited, but never heard anything else. At that distance, he couldn't even guess at the size of the dueling bucks.

Frustrated, he slowly returned to his original position and rested the back of his head against the tree trunk. His right leg was cramping now, and his toes were no longer aching but throbbing. He curled his toes in his boots and kept working them to help blood circulate. His eyes were shut but he was wide-awake, letting his ears see and feel for him. There was no way he was leaving now.

From experience, he knew the only way to forget about the aching in his feet and legs were to withdraw into his mind. Like many other times, he began to think about things he'd done or would like to have done; things he had done that maybe shouldn't have been done.

After his Alaskan life had lost its glitter, he traveled to New Orleans and worked at a shipyard for several years. The work was agreeable, but the humid heat wore a man out. Like many young men, he'd often seek refuge in a local neighborhood bar, which had plenty of cold beer and cold air for those with enough pocket change. When he and one of his dockworker buddies were invited to a speakeasy to play poker one Friday night, Melvin jumped at the chance. A poker player by nature, Melvin liked the strategy in the game. They left the High & Low Bar immediately.

He and his friend had been playing for several hours when a card player he didn't know accused the house of using marked cards. Melvin didn't disagree; he'd thought it was odd that when he had a flush, one or another of the players would have a full house, or when he had three of a kind, another player would have a straight. It was stranger still that this only happened with there was a big pot. But Melvin, being a newcomer, hadn't yet worked up enough courage—or perhaps ire—to speak his suspicions aloud. This other fella had.

When the man accused the house of cheating, a fight broke out, and the accuser was cut deep. Melvin and his friend got in a couple of licks before they escaped the melee and returned to the High & Low. They were sitting at the bar when two husky police officers appeared, and questioned Melvin and his friend. The bartender piped up and said, "No, officers, you must be mistaken. They've been in my bar for two straight hours." The policemen walked out and never returned.

All I got for my trouble was bruised ribs and a hundred dollars short, Melvin thought with a grin. *But I did thank the barkeep for bailing me out.*

* * *

While at the High & Low, Melvin met a woman. She waited on tables there. Mae was a woman with eyes like an emerald sea and hair as black as coal. Mae had a child, a little girl, and her husband had run out on them when Mae was twenty-one, right after the baby came.

The child was fragile, had terrible bouts with breathing, and when the little girl was three, she got pneumonia and died. Melvin had grown fond of the child and took her death hard. He paid for most of the funeral arrangements, but it wasn't enough to ease the ache of loss.

After that, Mae's moods swung from one extreme to another. She started singing out and talking to herself, and couldn't remember things like she used to. It frightened Melvin so, he eventually stopped seeing her. It wasn't that he didn't feel sorry for her; he did. He couldn't imagine her grief. If it had been his child, he would have probably gone nuts, too.

Maybe that's why God didn't let me have children. Maybe He knew if I lost my child, I couldn't bear it. Where do parents get the strength to live with that kind of pain and loss? I bet it's faith and hope in the divine promise of life after death. I hope there's life after this world, anyway.

But if it ain't got places like swamps, I might not wanna go.

Chapter 12

He opened his eyes and moved them to the right, then to the left. *I know there's a heaven, because I've walked, touched and felt it right here. Only God could have created such a place as this.*

He breathed in the cold air and exhaled. Only a foolish hunter would be out in this kind of cold. *Even that big old buck is probably laughing. I bet that buck is watching me, thinking what a stupid man I am.* He shivered, and then murmured, "I *am* freezing to death." Again he wondered how much longer he could take the cold.

He heard something. When the noise came again, he looked to his left and saw a beaver easing out of the water. He watched it muff up its fur, lick its legs, essentially grooming itself.

The Melvin extended both legs to force better circulation to his feet. For the next few minutes, he quarreled with himself about going back to the camp. Then he leaned his head against the oak and shut his eyes.

In the far distance, he heard a train bellowing like a lonely bull in a pasture. He heard squirrels barking, an occasional owl in the distance, rushing water, the infrequent whistle of a wood duck, an intermittent bird, and the roaring made by the train heading north.

He drifted while in a half snooze—he couldn't recall the time, or if maybe he'd read it instead—when a Creek Indian said that for a man to be at peace with himself, he must first be at peace with nature. Then it came to his mind: He hadn't read it, a Creek Indian really *had* told him, that time he and Martha floated the Escambia River from Alabama to where it empties into Pensacola Bay.

They were like kids: talked, laughed, fished, cut up, pushed each other out of the boat, camped on sugar-white sandbars, and swam naked in the water. At night, they talked until the campfire dimmed. On those nights, the stars were so close, you could have reached out one hand and grabbed one. It took them nearly two weeks to make the journey down the river to the bay. By the end of the trip, both of them had a case of homesickness.

Martha loved her flowerbeds and her little garden. She grew all kinds of flowers, but he couldn't recall all the names. When he was younger, their names meant little to him.

Now it's different, the way I see the world. When Martha was alive, all I could see was "a flower" and "a tree." Age does that to a man, changes his priorities, and makes him contemplate things. Now I see joy in a flower and the miraculous in things.

Maybe that change began from knowing Martha. He recalled their first home: a two bedroom, one-bath A-frame, but it was the biggest castle in the world to them. Martha could cook, knew how to prepare the best meals he'd ever eaten. *A man's meal*, he would tell her, teasing. Meals that was especially good when she brought them to the work site where he was.

Whenever he'd been working for two or three weeks straight, she made him take off for a long weekend so they could get away together. They went to Atlanta, to the zoo, to the movies, and ate out for every meal. Other times, they'd rent a cottage on the Gulf, relax and fish.

Even there, Martha liked order, and when he got too relaxed in his ways, she'd call him on it. She had a place where all work clothes and boots belonged, and there was no exception. When she got mad, the tip of her nose would turn red and her hazel eyes garden-green. And she did have a temper. Their disputes were many, about business and other things. Once, she threw his boots at him for not putting them in the place they belonged. When she did, he turned her over his lap, threatening to spank her if she didn't settle down.

He was fighting a memory-induced chuckle when he heard the sound. He opened his eyes and held his breath, listening, cursing the noise of the rising water and the train off in the distance for muddling the sound.

No more sound came, but he moved his eyes back and forth, sure he'd heard something. There were no movements or objects out of place as he investigated everything within his view with all his senses.

Even the tiniest object was scrutinized carefully. *It's the tiny things and small objects that lead to the big prize.* Thinking it might have been the boar cat squirrel he saw earlier, he looked at the ground beneath the big oak. The squirrel was no longer there.

The train was gone; all he could hear now was running water, too loud, but in tempo with the environment. Yet he knew something was out of sync. To him, it was as obvious as a split reed on a clarinet. *It's a buck . . . a big one, too. Maybe it's the big bruiser I'm after. Gawd, if I could only see it! I know it's there!*

He fought to remain motionless lest his body betray his location. His heart pumped under his camouflage coveralls, but he no longer felt cold: no throbbing toes and his fingers seemed thawed when he moved them.

Then it came again, barely audible—the sound most hunters ignored or confused with another voice, like one might confuse the tone of a trumpet with that of a coronet. It took years, if ever, to truly recognize this sound.

* * *

Melvin couldn't remember how many years passed before he discovered the voice a deer has. He'd heard it for years, but shrugged it off until one afternoon when he watched a deer travel within ten steps of him. Since then, he'd seen and heard deer making that sound for years. *What a prized piece of information for a deer hunter*, he'd thought many times since. *Like reading top-secret information about your enemy.* Everyone knew that a deer snorts, blows, stomps its feet, grunts and bleats, but not everyone knew the voice a deer mimics. The sound, once recognized, could never be forgotten. The voice a deer mimics is so prized, it's like drawing four of a kind in a card game.

He wondered if Indians knew about a deer's secretive expression, and if they did, if they had ever shared it. Likely not—Melvin hadn't, not with anyone. He'd hunted with one other hunter he suspected was aware of the voice, but he wasn't sure. And Melvin sure wasn't going to ask him. If he did, the secret would no longer be a secret. Melvin was usually happy to share other hunting techniques, especially deer-hunting methods. Not this one.

Once, while with this hunter, Melvin asked him about the various sounds deer made. He never mentioned the specific voice. The other hunter only gave Melvin an evasive smile, and Melvin never mentioned it again to him, or anyone else. Why share a secret that can only be earned? But now he wanted to share this information with one person—Chad—the next time he came up to hunt. He didn't know why he'd waited so long, but there was time to do that.

He was shivering, but the excitement of hearing the voice emboldened him, made him believe a buck was near. *I'll give it another thirty minutes*, he thought, knowing that he'd give it a lot more if his instincts kept telling him to stay.

The longbow rested on his lap. He reached down, but couldn't feel it. His fingers throbbed now, and if that buck walked in range, he might not be able to pull or feel the string. He'd felt worse pain, but what he felt now reminded him of getting his fingers caught in a car door. He must warm his fingers.

The deer blind concealed his movements and most of the sounds he was making. He hoped. He pulled off the gloves and blew air onto his hands, then made fists and put them between his legs, all the time watching and listening. After a moment, he blew into the gloves several times, then slid them back on. His fingers felt warm again.

He sat looking straight ahead, only shifting his eyes from left to right occasionally. A splashing noise came from behind him, but he didn't flinch; it was either wood ducks dropping out of the sky or a beaver. Or maybe an otter.

Then it came again. He waited, listening. His heart was revving, yet his breathing was calm. The shivering was involuntary.

In front of him, he saw two cardinals fly onto a branch three feet above the ground. He allowed his attention to stray to them. *What a handsome bird, the red bird. A blue bird is just as beautiful.* In fact, he couldn't think of a bird that was ugly, except maybe the buzzard. *But even turkey buzzards are useful birds.*

The noise returned, and his attention returned. A raccoon sow with two small cubs came wobbling by on the slough bank, their fur muffed and matted. He watched them groom themselves, wondering why they would swim the slough to get over to this island when they could have crossed on the foot log.

Judging by the sun, more than thirty minutes had passed when he finally leaned his head back against the tree and shut his eyes. *I can't remember it being this cold. Maybe I* should *hang it up for this evening and start fresh in the morning.*

Then, it came again. He looked straight in front of him, then moved his eyes side to side slowly. Again the soft noise almost like someone coughed. But it was *closer this time.*

He eased his right hand across his lap and removed the glove, gripped the arrow where it was nocked and started working his left hand toward the center of the bow.

The sound repeated itself, and seemed stronger. Even closer than before. *It's a deer . . . no doubt about it now.*

He shifted his weight to his right side and positioned the bow on his lap to better see the arrow and nock. He quickly glanced at the bow and arrow. The arrow was firmly on the string, in the right spot.

When the noise came again, the only thing that moved was his chest . . . at first. Without blinking or moving his head, he looked to the right and stared until his peripheral vision blurred the background with grayish spots.

A wood thrasher flew low to the ground from the swamp briars, making its muted cough, a cardinal and wren followed. He looked for any movement: a white patch, a leg, something that might be part of a deer.

Just then, he saw a black object vanish. It *was* a deer,

and big—as big as that old buck he was after. But maybe not the buck. He wondered why a swamp deer had darker hair, nearly black-looking, than a deer that remained on the hillside in the pines and oaks. Maybe the hill deer got more sunlight than the swamp deer did. He moved his eyes with concentration.

The earlier sounds of the swamps were gone, as were the raccoons. He never saw them leave. He sensed a big animal was in the vicinity. Institutively, he felt something looking at him. *I must remain motionless, like a tree. Can't get careless. I'm too close now.*

As long as he kept them behind the ground stand, he could move his hands without being seen. He was relieved when he slowly made a fist and his fingers still felt warm.

The voice came again and he kept shifting his eyes, searching the area for anything out of place, noting that the sun was sinking behind the ridge. *My luck to see the big buck today and kill it in this weather.* He began to think about how he would get the buck back to the main house before dark.

The sound came again, but the sound was moving away. *Maybe it's feeding. Maybe. Or maybe it's checking this ground stand out. Whatever it's doing, it's still close.*

In the distance a trail dog barked and he could barely hear it. But he'd seen something—that flash of black as it disappeared—and that gave him hope.

A group of wood ducks lifted off the darkening water,

whistling as they went. *Probably going to roost. Or maybe they saw something, too. But they don't usually get alarmed at a deer. Maybe a coyote.*

He glanced at the slough; the water was encroaching faster. Thirty minutes at most, and he'd have to leave for the camp house.

A gasp escaped his lips when he saw a rack, then the body of a buck emerge from the thick undergrowth. The buck walked with its head down, feeding on acorns. In the instant it took Melvin to realize it wasn't his trophy, the buck had vanished.

Just then, limbs popped and broke; a heavy running thud exploded from beneath a treetop lying on the ground eighty steps in front. Out charged an enormous buck with a huge webbed rack and a scooped-out gully in its snout. At last, the hunter had Mossback in sight.

Chapter 13

The giant buck went straight for the young buck feeding on acorns.

Melvin's three fingers gripped the nock and arrow. He barely felt the bowstring. Melvin could have shot, probably should have, but halted when he saw the younger buck lower its antlers and the monster buck rear up on its hind legs, rocking its antlers, moving its hooves up and down, threatening, attempting to walk on its hind legs, hopping and bobbing toward the younger buck. Upright on its hind legs, the buck looked about twelve feet tall.

Through the big, moss-laden trees, Melvin watched the small buck wheel around, and bounced twenty, maybe thirty feet and stop beside a tree trunk. The young buck looked back at the giant buck.

The giant buck took the challenge. Without hesitation, it came down on its front two legs and charged after the smaller buck. Mossback ran straight and steady, his head low to the ground.

To Melvin, the buck's antlers looked unnatural with their wide beams and tall spikes. Those antlers seemed motionless as the big buck charged across the flats toward the young buck, his mossy-furred back blending in with the shrouded trees around him.

The young buck took off and bounced in a small circle, dogging trees and vines, then wheeled in an instant and came bouncing toward the ground stand where Melvin sat watching and waiting.

Without thinking, Melvin squeezed the arrow nock and drew the string to his chest. *Don't move, he's coming. Be still, old man, he's coming.*

Melvin wasn't referring to the buck bouncing in his direction, but to the one just behind him. Mossback would be drawn by the younger buck's behavior like a hornet to a swatting hand.

He kept his eyes nailed to the two bucks as Mossback charged close enough for him to better see the deep, scooped-out pit in the buck's snout. In long, long strides, the big buck was coming closer to his stand.

The younger buck bounded within twenty steps of the front of the camouflaged stand, then traveled another forty, maybe fifty feet, and stopped then looked back at the giant buck. As soon as the young buck stopped, Mossback stopped.

This is what Melvin had practiced and prayed for the last four years. In one fluid motion, he rose up from his seated position, reaching full draw with the string at the same time. At twenty paces, the arrowhead's journey would be exact and deadly.

The bow-limbs moaned when he released the string at the precise moment that Mossback looked toward the ground stand. The arrow struck with a smacking sound and the big buck dropped in its tracks, broken down in the back, swiveling its head wildly, plowing the soft ground with its front legs. In hurried excitement, the younger buck took off, then stopped, looked back for a second, then bounced out of sight.

* * *

Melvin watched Mossback's efforts to stand. It wobbled, trembled, then its hind legs collapsed and the buck dropped down into the mud and leaves with its front legs spread out ahead of him.

Melvin eased back down on the bucket, his fingers throbbing from the string. But those were his only discomforts. He was still cold, but didn't shiver or tremble as he had moments before. No, he remained calm and just watched the huge buck he'd been hunting for four years.

Melvin paid little attention to his surroundings or to anything else. The struggling monster on the ground had all his attention. Without realizing he was doing so, he pulled on his gloves. *What an evening this is going to be.* After that? He didn't want to think that far ahead, just savor the moment.

Every minute or two, looking bewildered, the buck made an effort to stand. But each time, its muscled hindquarters trembled, shook, and then collapsed beneath its body.

One thing Melvin detested, and the last thing he wanted to happen, was maiming the buck. He couldn't see where the arrowhead had stuck the animal, but the arrow must have hit the buck's spine; the feathered fletching and splintered shaft of the arrow was on the ground beside the buck's hindquarters. He was dumbfounded when he saw the location of the arrow, but content. It made no difference now where the flint point had hit; the buck was mortally wounded, and Melvin knew it.

Patience had value and paid great dividends. Patience was a prized asset in a situation like this. But time was a liability now. The sunlight would soon play out, and it would be dark. Melvin debated with himself about waiting ten minutes to let the buck calm down and bleed out. But the right thing to do was waiting, he knew.

What mattered most now was allowing the buck to die naturally. He didn't want to deprive it of its right to die with honor and dignity. Robbed of the quality of his own life, Melvin would want the same thing. He'd seen it firsthand, people and animals dying. They go into shock, lose consciousness, and die in peace without a sound. Nature had a benevolent side.

A part of him found it tough to watch the buck struggle, yet he still felt like he'd just made the winning touchdown in an important game. There were no handshakes, no pats on the butt, no congratulations. It was as if the fans were muted, hanging around like the Spanish moss, uninterested in the final outcome, just buoyed by knowing the ball was in the end zone.

Time went slowly as Melvin observed the buck's struggle. His lips moved, but no sound escaped from them.

The huge orange sun was sinking in the west like a feeling of dread when the phone rings late at night. Shafts of light speared through the vines and the tree trunks, softening them into chilly shadows.

Even though it couldn't remain standing, the buck didn't seem any weaker after five minutes. He still looked strong and weary-wild, like a highly prized racehorse that had come up lame and wanted to desperately run.

Not being able to stand on your legs frustrates, Melvin thought. He believed he understood the frustration. On rare occasions, his legs cramped up at night, and he could barely stand. He'd take an aspirin, and in the morning his legs would be fine.

But a deer won't understand why he can't get up. Even one this smart.

The buck made another attempt to stand. Again Melvin watched it rear up on its front legs, pulling its body forward with its back legs dragging. Finally, it hit him: the buck was trying to get to the water, which had risen even more and moved so fast now it made a roaring sound like a distant train.

Deer were like any other animal when wounded—they headed for water. He'd seen wounded deer get into water and lay down. He'd seen wounded deer get into water over their heads and sink to the bottom, as if preferring to drown rather than let the hunter take them.

What wild and unbelievable things deer do?

145

He admired deer for not being taken without a fight, but this fight, he wanted no part of. In spite of its injury, this deer was big, mean, and strong.

The deer's shoulders strained against its massive weight as it knifed toward the water. This time, it made it about ten feet on its front hooves before it collapsed in the wet leaves and mud, then it looked to the right, and then left, away from Melvin.

Each time the buck looked away, it held its head still, seeming to scan in the direction of the thicket. The buck did this several times, acting as if ready to challenge something in the undergrowth. The buck didn't appear to see Melvin, or even care he was there. Melvin wondered what was in the thicket that seemed to have spooked the buck.

Maybe it's another hunter, trespassing?

Melvin watched the thicket. The more he watched, the more certain he became that the buck was anxious about something in the thicket. *If he's worried, maybe I should be worried, too.*

Melvin observed the buck's curved ears stand up, rotate and appear to listen intently in the direction of the thicket. He strained to hear and looked carefully at the dark shadows for any unusual movement, but saw and heard nothing.

The buck reared up again, and this time made it close—too close—to the water's edge.

"Damn, I should have brought another arrow," Melvin

muttered. "I need to finish you off before you get to the water. My luck to stick you and you get away."

Melvin heard a soft crack and a rustling in the thicket and the sounds were unnatural. Didn't fit. Like a bump in the night, noises you can hear but can't determine its origin or understand the meaning.

The sound worried him, gave him the gut-twisting feeling you get in a public place that you're being watched. A warning sound drowned by the roaring water. He strained to listen for the sound to come again.

Maybe it's blue jays. They can mimic other birds. Maybe animals too?

The sunlight made a faint glittering on the thicket, blue-white on the ice that had begun to re-form on the tree limbs. Time was growing shorter. *Whatever I'm gonna do, gotta be done fast,* he thought. *Time is never a friend.*

He stood quietly and leaned his longbow against the stand beside the quiver, then opened the framed gate on his ground stand, walked through it, and closed it firmly without a sound.

Crouching, he made a wide half-circle, keeping the massive tree trunk between him and the buck. He was glad it was distracted by something in the thicket. He could barely feel his toes in his blasted rubber boots, so he stopped behind the tree trunk and shifted his feet around in the boots so he could move more stealthily.

Then it came: a noise from the shadows in the thicket.

He strained to listen, but the once-lethargic moving water roared like a smooth-running engine over the beaver dam. He waited several minutes, motionless, looking and listening as he watched the buck's ears flipping and rotating side to side.

Maybe I didn't hear anything, he decided. *But I got to get moving.*

The buck's web rack looked strong, menacing and arrogant. Melvin counted nineteen points, and the beam was at least three feet across. He estimated the animal's weight at 320, maybe 345 pounds. The longest spine on the antler went up and curved forward; it was maybe fourteen inches. The flat web rack was at least ten, maybe twelve inches wide, with spikes eight inches high, maybe ten. The spikes went straight up, like fingers on a man's hand. He counted ten spikes that budded out into smaller points. The circumference of the beams at the buck's head looked the size of a grown man's forearm. A rack like that could pin another buck to the ground, or him if he got close enough.

As before, the deer's front legs were splayed in front of its body, but now its large eyes were wild, strange. Even so, they looked cold and unafraid. *Calculating.*

The buck tilted its antlers at an angle that seemed to signal *Come forward, old man.* Melvin understood the message; he'd seen a poker stare more than once.

The buck's eyes were brown-black, and a hint of lime green showed in the pupils. Melvin had seen this greenish look in a deer's eyes before, and often wondered why their pupils were this way when they were dying or dead.

Maybe it's nature's angry soul, he thought. *But, nature doesn't have a soul, except the one I rode on the Colorado River.*

It came to his mind that the buck's eyes were evaluating alternatives, and the risks of each outcome. A thousand-yard stare: cold, blank, showing only the absence of a soul.

Its eyes are asking me to raise the stakes or fold. The realization surprised him at first, and then made him angry.

He pointed at the buck. "If I had my pistol, I'd *stop* that stare," he said. "I have to finish you off now, and all I have is a knife. There's no honor in a pistol, but a knife's not much better. If I come near you, you'll fight me anyway. But if I leave you alone to get the pistol, you might drag yourself into the water."

With every passing minute, Melvin was thinking, and his thoughts led him to an idea, something he'd done before. The knife was no good, since Mossback would likely attack him as soon as he got close enough.

But he had enough time to walk back to the camp and get his .38, then come back and finish the job before dark. He could tie its paralyzed back legs to a tree! That would keep the deer in one place long enough for him to walk out and come back with his pistol.

But there was so little time before dark. "Wish I'd

brought the pistol with me," he said, his voice a frustrated moan. "Or even another arrow. Dammit to hell!"

Melvin removed the nylon cord from his jacket with shivering, cold-numbed fingers and attempted to tie a knot on both ends, to make a lasso with a noose that would remain tied. Each time, he failed.

It was like trying to tie a knot in a piece of thread with one's fingers encased in thick gloves. The thought startled him, and he looked at his hands, laughing. "'Course you can't tie a lasso, fool," he yelped. "Not with these rawhide gloves!"

Still chuckling, he knelt down to steady himself, then placed the tip of his glove in his teeth and pulled until the glove slid off. The other one followed soon after.

He cupped his hands as if he were going to pray, then placed them over his mouth and blew warm air from deep in his lungs. The pain in his left side came back, but only for a moment.

He rubbed his hands together several times, but his next attempt to make a lasso also failed. His hands, numbed from the cold and calloused from years of hard work, simply wouldn't cooperate.

"Damn it," he said, softly this time, and then glanced at the buck's eyes. The buck had stopped struggling and was only staring at him now.

Melvin shivered. The buck's look was the kind you'd get from a barroom brawler: steady, stern and pissed-off.

"Maybe I *should* have brought my pistol," he whispered, "but you don't intimidate me. I'm not afraid of you."

The buck's eyes never moved; it just lay as if it was sunning itself on a hill, staring him down.

I know you're not in pain, Melvin thought, suddenly angry. *Your nervous system isn't like ours. I've seen an animal in pain or suffering. You're not in shock either, I can tell. Oh, why didn't I bring another arrow?* He glanced at the water, a rushing stream now. *In a couple of hours, the water might be one or two feet deep here, and it'll be pitch-dark. How stupid am I? I should have known better to come out here so late in the day!*

* * *

Finally, on his fifth attempt, the lasso appeared. When he stood, his legs cramped from the lack of circulation. He pulled on the gloves, keeping his eyes on the buck the whole time.

His face felt like he'd had a shot of Novocain. He experienced no sensation in it. He breathed deep, and again felt the sharp pinch inside his ribs. But when he exhaled slowly, he felt nothing except the flushing pain of the feeling returning to his face.

Holding the lasso up like a spoil of war, Melvin spoke to the buck. "Ole boy, I know how dangerous your species can be when wounded . . . and how dangerous your species can be when *not* wounded. Nature gave you that much. If you heave yourself up on your front legs and start for the water or me, I won't have the strength to stop you."

He dropped his arm beside him. The lasso slapped his thigh, but he didn't feel it. "You're drawing a flush. I'm drawing three of a kind. And you know it, don't you?"

He knew the buck was territorial and would fight to the death. Once, he'd had a dog killed by a deer. He'd seen them chase marauding packs of coyotes around and around and whip them all. No, Melvin didn't want to get between the buck and the water. He'd seen them lie in water with only their snouts exposed, waiting.

Deer were smart and clever, a cleverness that made him believe deer could think. Deer used their superior sight and smell to their advantage, too. He'd seen deer walk within thirty or forty yards of a hunter, and the hunter never saw the deer. The deer's fur didn't reflect light; instead, it absorbed light. He'd seen deer walk into the shade of a tree and vanish. He'd seen deer lay motionlessness and let a hunter walk past. Other times, the hunter would jump a doe, she'd run off, and the buck would remain, invisible.

He took the lasso and opened it so it formed a narrow noose. When he pulled on the main rope, the noose would close tight. The buck's head crane slowly until the gully in its snout was positioned over its left shoulder. Just like it had decided to give up and was beckoning him to put the noose around its neck.

Melvin gave the buck another respectful smile. *Yep, fooling around with a wounded buck is playing Russian roulette with five rounds in the cylinder.*

He wouldn't go anywhere near the buck's still-functioning wide head or front legs. Instead, he would use the lasso to tie the back legs together, like handcuffs, then tie the rope to a tree so the big buck wouldn't heave itself up and attack him or make it to the water.

He knew he couldn't stop the buck if it decided to leave, but if it charged him, Melvin was pretty sure he could maneuver around the trees fast enough to keep the buck off him.

He moved toward the buck, keeping his pace slow and even. For the first time, he was able to see the entrance wound. He didn't see the flint arrowhead. Surprisingly, he saw no grievous wound, and little blood. He had suspected this.

The main artery was below the backbone. If the artery were severed, the buck would now be in shock, nearing death from blood loss. Even if the artery had just been nicked, it would have already weakened the buck more than this.

I wonder if his back is fractured or broke, or if the arrow just stunned him.

The buck slowly moved one of its hind legs. Seeing this, he knew the buck's spinal cord wasn't cut or seriously damaged. Yet he didn't jump back at the realization. His coolness came from years of experience. He'd killed lots of big bucks. But his calm was in peril. He was in danger of being attacked by an angry buck, and he knew it.

He heard no sounds other than the thumping of his heart. *I wonder what an Indian would do.*

Melvin believed a primal instinct to kill the weaker is inbred in all animals. But the instinct to survive is mightier than the instinct to kill for food. In a fight for survival, fear is the major shareholder of strength and courage. Melvin knew this firsthand.

He'd read about a lion on the Serengeti Plain in Africa being fatally wounded and still killing the hunter who shot it. He'd seen matadors on television being mauled and gored by a bull that was mortally wounded. He'd seen it happen in Texas when he was a cowboy: another cowboy getting gored and nearly dying.

He knew a deer hunter would risk life and limb to get a deer broken down. It made no difference where the deer traveled; as long as the hunter could track it, he'd never give up the hunt. He'd also read about deer hunters being badly hurt and even killed by a wounded buck. He'd go anywhere, too, for a deer, but he wasn't about to get into freezing water over his head. That would be total foolishness and he knew it. He had to keep the buck from the water.

With every passing moment, he felt his heart pumping faster, imagining all kinds of threats. He moved slowly, and only when necessary, because he didn't want to give the buck any notion that he was dangerous. But regardless, he couldn't back away. No matter how much he wanted to leave to think this through, it was too late. The sun was getting close to setting, and he was already too close to the animal. Time was running out, and darkness wouldn't wait on anything or anyone.

It'll only take a few seconds to get the noose around the two hooves, he thought to bolster himself. *Or if I could get one leg tied, that might be enough to secure him until I return.*

Still, he had to move slowly and on guard the entire time. He didn't want to startle or provoke the buck with a sudden move; all he wanted was to avoid eye contact with the buck and do what he needed to do to secure the buck in one quick motion.

He looked down at the powerful hindquarters. One leg was separated about six inches from the other, nearly like a thin Y. The top leg was slightly above the ground.

He eased down to a semi-squat. With every inch, his heart pounded harder. He carefully lowered the noose, and pulled the noose over the leg that was barely off the muddy leaves.

With two fingers, he brought the loop up the hindquarter, and then pulled it snug about ten inches up on the hind leg. He put slow pressure on the noose, and it held. Feeling relieved, he stepped back and tied the other end to an oak sapling about three inches in diameter. It was so easy; it was almost like the buck had expected it. *Allowed* it. He looked at the gigantic buck, which hadn't moved, and felt a sudden rush of sympathy.

Don't worry, Mossback. I won't leave you here long. I'll come back with my pistol or rifle and take you out before it gets too dark.

He backed up farther, avoiding eye contact with the buck, in hopes it would instinctively think the hunter didn't see him. If a deer thinks it can't be seen, it will remain motionless.

Nature made deer perfect against man and his senses, Melvin thought. *There's no match in a deer's environment. A deer wins ninety-nine percent of the time. But man is smarter and can think better most of the time.*

The buck jerked its upper body around and snorted several times, then made a gallant effort to stand, but the cord tightened on its hind leg. Then, as before, the legs shook and the buck collapsed. The buck looked at Melvin, gestured by moving its big wide head up and down, threatening, challenging him to bring it on.

Melvin backed farther away, ignoring the buck's eyes. He was now being doubled-teamed by the cold and adrenaline. He leaned against a tree, unzipped his overalls, and felt the warmth from his body rush up against his face. He took a deep breath. Again, he felt the pinch in his chest, this time along with an urge to cough. The feeling went away when he swallowed several times. He wiped his runny nose on his forearm and blinked against the sudden moisture in his eyes, then tried to think of the best way back to the camp house.

The muddy water was out of the banks around the slough and had encroached even farther, four, maybe six inches, possibly high enough to cover the foot log when he got to it. He didn't look forward to the prospect of wading across the running water. With all his hunting clothes on, if he fell in the freezing water over his head, he'd probably drown. But there was no choice; he had to make it to the camp house and back before dark.

Careful not to step on sticks or limbs, and to keep the buck from being alarmed by his movement, he walked slowly through the mud to his ground stand, removed his longbow and quiver. He turned and looked back at the enormous buck lying on the ground. The antlers were the first things he saw.

What a beautiful animal, he thought, then waded through the water that was flooding the bottoms.

* * *

The dingy water went above his ankles, and his boots made squashing sounds when he took a step. As he suspected it would, the water lapped at the top of the foot log.

He'd crossed the foot log a hundred times before, but this time he felt nervous enough to stop and survey the log before stepping onto it. There was nothing to anchor the old, likely porous old tree against floating, and he knew he'd be in trouble if the log rolled and he fell in the water. The slough was over his head now, and he wasn't sure if he could make it out if he fell. With one careful step after another, he was on the other side of the slough before he had a chance to think much more about it.

He looked back through the trees and vines and saw the buck looking in the direction of the thicket. Melvin stared at the undergrowth for a minute or two. Seeing nothing, he proceeded up the hill.

* * *

By the time he reached the top of the ridge, he was breathing heavily and had to lean against a tree to catch his breath. It took far too many minutes for him to be able to restart his stumbling walk.

They were right, he thought, *I'm too old.*

A few minutes more, he was on the game path, out of sight of the buck, headed to the camp house. If he kept making good time, perhaps darkness wouldn't create another problem. To do what he had to do, he needed the daylight. As he walked, he mulled over his plan.

A small branch whipped back and stung his ear.

"Damn!"

He stopped, grabbed his earlobe and shook his head. The best word to describe the pain was a wasp sting on your ear. Only outdoorsmen know of this pain and the intensity of the short-lived suffering.

He stopped to rest against a tree. Except for the muffled but labored roar made by the water, there was absolute stillness. The sky, though fading, was pale blue, and the air was fresh, clean and frigid.

After catching his breath, he headed toward the camp. Aside from the approaching dark, he had a gnawing in his gut. An urgency. He didn't understand it but he felt uneasy, anxious. Almost like a tug of guilt that drew him faster down the brush-choked path.

Several hundred yards later, he was breathing like a long-distance runner crossing the finish line. He stopped and leaned against a tree, letting gravity take him to a sitting position as he looked in the direction of the low sun. The starved-looking clouds seemed in need of more volume. The air seemed thin, harder to inhale than before.

"Hold on," he breathed into the air, making puffs with his words. "Not too much longer."

After several minutes, he was able to continue walking toward the cabin. The path got wider and he knew it was a hundred yards before he reached the lane, then a couple hundred yards more to the camp house.

Chapter 14

Back at the camp house, shadows were darker and the dirt had thawed into slush. He leaned the longbow against the wall and attempted to turn the doorknob, but his hands were like blocks of ice. He swore, and after a few tries, he opened the door and went in, leaving it open.

He hadn't known peace since he saw the buck. Warmth, either. In a hurry, he retrieved a box of matches and, after several attempts, lit the heater. Holding his palms out to the flames, his fingers thawed like water in a frozen pipe. The heater roared as it filled the cabin with warmth.

After closing the door, he lit the eye on the stove and placed a kettle of water on. He didn't regret the time—perhaps hot coffee and getting warm would make his return journey faster. He paced around the kitchen, thinking what to bring back to the swamps. The whole time, he kept an eye on the position of the sun.

The water was taking too long to boil. He paced and the floors creaked and groaned under his weight. He peeked out the door and looked around a moment. When he looked back, the kettle was pouring steam. He was right; from the first mouthful of coffee, he felt better.

He removed all his wet hunting clothes and piled them in the corner, then leaned his rubber boots against the wall away from the heater. In the bedroom, he pulled on a dry pair of insulated camouflage overalls over his long johns.

The clothing felt warm on his body, but he resisted the urge to add more. *Shouldn't dress heavy. I'll be plenty warm carrying the buck.*

He hung the empty quiver on a nail and looked at it a moment. The hawk's tail feather was spinning slowly, but the quiver didn't look the same without the handmade arrow. The longbow he leaned against the wall in the far corner. That would keep the heater's heat from warping it while it thawed out.

He glanced at the window again. *So little time.*

Back in his room, he located the 38-caliber pistol and quickly checked the cylinder. There were six rounds nestled in it. As he snapped the cylinder back into place, he thought about taking his rifle back with him. But it was cold, and the rifle would get wet. Just another heavy object to carry. As much as he objected to finishing the buck off with a gun, he knew he had no other option. The knife would have been too dangerous. At least the pistol was lightweight.

He hadn't fired the .38 in a while, so he hurried outside and down the steps, aimed it at the ground and fired. The sound went a long way and echoed for a while.

Inspiration struck him, and he laid the pistol at the corner of the porch and went inside the house. In another bedroom, he slid a box from beneath a cot, placed the box on the cot and opened it. He removed a pair of chest waders, took them into the kitchen and placed them on the table.

The clock told him he had to hurry with his plan. He went outside, down the steps and walked over to the small, enclosed shed where the canoe was located.

The old shed always had a smell of oil, grease and fuel, but it was neat, with tools generally located in a specific spot. The noise he made moving things around packed the air with clangs and thuds as he examined the green and brown-spotted, twelve-foot metal canoe. When he reached the bow and saw the hole Chad had told him about, he winced.

He knew from experience that his weight would probably keep the bow out of the water, away from the hole. But even if he waded next to the canoe most of the way, he couldn't be sure with the buck's added weight.

The hole was about the size of a man's hand. He could plug it. Even a temporary patch would work, at least to slow down a water leak. After all, the channel was the deep part, and it was only about twenty or thirty feet across. With the chest waders, he could wade the rest of the way out.

He dragged the canoe out of the shed and rolled it over, then went back in the shed for a hammer and nails. Laying them aside, he placed a small sheet of quarter-inch plywood in his vise, and used his handsaw to cut two eight-inch-rectangular pieces. He took one of the pieces to the canoe and placed the plywood over the hole. With a pencil, he outlined the hole on the piece of wood, and returned to the shed.

He laid the piece with its outline on top of the other rectangle, and drove nails through both, nailing both pieces together. He took the claw hammer and removed the nails. Now, all he had to do was match the holes up on either side of the canoe, tap a nail through them, and bend the nails with the hammer. To seal around the holes, he took some black electrical tape and a screwdriver.

After he finished hammering the rectangles in place, he used the screwdriver to push strips of tape between the wood and metal on both sides. The tape acted like corking. It would leak some, but he didn't have a long way to travel across the slough. He was confident the temporary patch would hold long enough for him to float the buck out to Fannie Road.

The thirty minutes invested in repairing the canoe would pay off in an easier return trip, and actually took less time than he thought. He had time for a quick supper.

He pulled the canoe to the back of his truck and let the tailgate down, then returned to the kitchen for a supper of a baloney sandwich, unheated pork and beans from a can eaten with a plastic spoon, and a soft drink.

He could have any kind of food he wanted, but he was never impressed by fancy meals. Especially now, when all he needed was food for energy to get him through the next few hours. With every passing minute, he imagined he was taking too long to eat.

He inspected his hunting gear neatly placed on the

table, and thought he was still missing something. Chiding himself, he walked over to the pile of wet hunting clothes on the floor and retrieved his belt, the knife and scabbard. He went out the door, got his pistol and brought it back to the table.

After a last slug of coffee, he rested the cup on the table while he took all his gear and put it in the front seat of the truck. The sixty-pound canoe went up easily into the truck's bed. He got in the truck and cranked it. When he was sure the idle was smooth, he returned to the house for a final check.

There was mud on the porch and in the kitchen. He'd clean it up later. He turned off the heater and checked to make sure the stove was off. He still kept thinking he'd forgotten something. But he had plenty: his pistol, knife, chest waders, canoe, flashlight, cord, and gloves. And the canoe.

What else could there be? Just nerves, you old man. Quit stalling. If you leave now, you'll be home right around dark, or near to it. He made sure the porch light was on, and went to the shed and shoved the door closed. No need to have a raccoon family take over while he was gone.

He was walking back to the trunk when he hesitated a moment with the same notion; he was leaving something important behind. *The boat paddle!* After he retrieved the hand-carved paddle from the shed, he was finally speeding down the lane.

When he arrived at the place where the lane met the path, he stopped and unloaded the canoe, then put all his gear in it. He drove down the lane where it merged into Fannie Road, then drove down Fannie Road to Flat Creek Bridge.

He'd meant to park the truck there, but when he saw the water was about two inches below the bridge, he changed his mind. After some doing, he turned the truck around and drove about a hundred yards above the bridge to an incline, a place where there was no danger of the truck getting flooded. The keys went on the floorboard: no chance of losing them in the channel this way.

He rushed up Fannie Road to where he left the canoe. Each minute decreased the daylight and added a minute to dark.

He looked at the orange skullcap behind the trees. In the distance, he heard dueling owls; they seemed to be starting early this evening. In the east was a barely visible white moon. He gave one more thought to what he might have left, but only as a way of putting the worry to rest. *It's a damn shame if I left something*, he thought, *but it's too late now*.

He hung the chest waders over his shoulders, put the pistol and flashlight in his pockets, and checked again to make sure he had his knife, cord and paddle. He heaved the canoe up and rested it on his back.

As he traveled along the path, he considered going at

least a couple of hundred yards on the ridge above the foot log. From there he could drift quietly down the slough to the spot where the buck was. It might keep the buck from being spooked with the noise of him coming down the ridge with the canoe at the foot log. That spot was too close to the buck.

* * *

Halfway down the game path now, and making pretty good time. He'd stopped several times to rest and to pee. Now he stood and rested a moment more while looking up the path he would travel, then heaved the canoe onto his shoulders and started down the path.

He was breathing heavily, but not as heavy as he had earlier. He didn't feel as cold as before, either. His nose and face were cold, but his hands felt good inside the gloves. Occasionally the canoe banged into a small tree or brush, or limbs raked along the canoe with a *zing* or *zip* or growling noise. There were no more shadows, but plenty of light remained.

After a short time, he stopped to rest again. He let the canoe slide off his shoulders to the ground with a metallic *thump*. As he straightened up, he stretched out his arms. Still about five football fields to travel before he'd be at the spot he wanted to be on the ridge. He was tired, but not done in. Plenty of energy left to do what he had to do.

As he stood on the path, he mulled over what he'd do when he got to the buck. First, he'd have to shoot and gut it. Then he'd put the deer in the canoe and float it across the channel. The final leg would be from there down to Fannie Road. His only concern was the channel, when he'd be wading beside the canoe; there were deep erosion ditches alongside the ridge, and he'd have to be careful to avoid falling into one of them. But that would only be for a short time. Once at Fannie Road, he could either load the buck in his truck or drag it back to the camp house.

After a few more minutes, he hoisted the canoe onto his shoulders and started down the path again.

Chapter 15

At the exact moment Melvin lifted the canoe, Chad was stopping his truck at Flat Creek Bridge. He had managed to get Beth to leave Pensacola early so he could come back to the camp before dark and hunt the remainder of the weekend with Melvin.

He saw Melvin's truck parked ahead on an incline and stopped, got out of his truck and walked in the mud to the bridge. The water was nearly even with the wood plank bridge, and had encroached about thirty yards onto Fannie Road. He returned to his truck and drove slowly across the bridge.

When he pulled alongside Melvin's truck, he stopped a moment to gaze at the dark trees that rose like steep cliffs in the swamps on both sides of the road. The muddy water crept up onto the flats.

Then he drove up Fannie Road to the lane and on to the camp house. There, he got out of his truck and took his gun case with him. Inside, he saw the mud scattered on the kitchen floor, Melvin's wet hunting clothes in a pile in the corner. He looked at the kitchen table and saw part of a baloney sandwich, a half-eaten can of pork and beans, a paper plate, and a coffee cup nearly full.

He glanced at the longbow and quiver, noted that the lone arrow no longer protruded from it, and he looked back at the counter and the sink. He went over to the kettle and held his hand slightly alongside it. Still warm.

"Dang it just missed him."

It was an unspoken rule, that one hunter never encroached on another hunter's business without being invited. Even if what the empty quiver implied was correct—that Uncle Melvin had gotten the buck he'd been talking about, or even gave it a damn good try and didn't—Chad owed it to him not to interfere on either his triumph, or his loss.

That didn't have to stop Chad from hunting, though. There was plenty of room for Uncle Melvin, him, and a hundred other hunters on the big spread, and they'd never even cross paths. Uncle Melvin would be back by dark—he always was—and they'd catch up then. And tomorrow, they would spend the day together.

Chad went into one of the bedrooms and changed into insulated hunting clothes. He removed his rifle from the gun case, walked outside and loaded it, got in the truck and drove around the camp house onto the small lane that went to the main farmhouse.

But he didn't go all the way there. When he reached the smallest field, he stopped. The small clearing that went along the path to the swamps would be a good place to hunt deer.

Rifle in hand, he climbed on the back of the truck and sat on the toolbox. As he sat there, only his eyes moving just like his uncle had taught him when he was five, Chad made plans to fulfill Uncle Melvin's request to clear the field.

* * *

About the time Chad was resting his butt on the toolbox, Melvin let the canoe slide off his shoulders at the spot on the ridge he'd wanted to end up. After a few minutes, he started down the slope, trying to be quiet as he dragged the canoe behind him.

At the water's edge, Melvin rested several minutes, then stripped off his insulated camouflage coveralls and pulled on the chest waders. He put his knife scabbard in a brown pouch inside the chest waders, the pouch he'd sewed into the chest waders to keep shotgun shells from getting wet when he duck hunted. Then he pulled the insulated coveralls back over the chest waders—a technique used by most experienced duck hunters.

After he finished changing clothes, he checked his gear. His pistol, knife, flashlight and cord were still with him. He looked at the water and saw foam and bits of wood drifting on top. *If I didn't know the area, I sure wouldn't want to step into that!* He thought with a grin.

He slid the canoe in the water and waded alongside it. The slough channel was about twenty yards ahead and well over his head now, so he waded beside the canoe for about ten yards, then got in and shoved the canoe with his leg toward the channel. He knelt inside the canoe to check the temporary patch he made earlier. As he predicted, it was above the waterline. He took the paddle, shoved it in the muddy water and pushed back and the canoe rocked and shot forward.

Nearing the channel, he felt the strength of the water as it pushed against the canoe. Again, he buried the paddle in the water and pushed back. The canoe went forward, and he steered the canoe on the surface of the once-sluggish water to the other side of the channel with unexpected ease. Here, where there was only swampy ground a few hours before, the water was about a foot deep and rising.

The slough had taken on the mature look of a fast-moving river. This concerned him a little, considering what the canoe would be carrying on its return trip.

He could hear the constant roar of water and the noise of rapids made by small sticks and logjams against the tree trunks—a sound he was familiar with from past floods. But during those, he'd been above the water, not in it.

As he started paddling downstream, the strong current pushed the canoe sideways into trees; then the canoe would get wedged between trees and brush. Each time, he stepped out of the canoe and waded beside it, steering it as he walked. Here, the water was halfway between his knee and ankle. A flock of wood ducks leaped off the water and flew at a forty-five degree angle through the trees, warning all who could hear.

He held out less hope now, but there was still a chance he could make it out before dark. The moon would be big and bright. That would help.

The sound came without warning. Startled, he stopped wading, and the current pushed the canoe into a tree trunk with a *bump*. He ignored it and strained to listen, worried.

Chapter 16

He looked around. The tree trunks were dark, and vines hung down from their limbs like gray-black ropes moving up and down in the water's current. Spanish moss that hung from limbs also rode on the surface, swaying back and forth like a witch's mane flying through the air.

He was sure he'd heard something, but he couldn't make any sense of it, or from what direction the sound came.

Baffled, he remained still, listening and watching. After a few minutes without hearing the noise again, he stepped back into the canoe and knelt down, then eased the paddle in the water to guide the canoe as it floated silently.

Afraid of making more noise than necessary, he took hold of a tree trunk and let the water's current pivot the front end of the canoe downstream. Still holding the tree, he pulled himself up. The canoe rocked against the current as he stepped in the knee-deep water.

He stopped. His senses were revved up. "I *know* I heard something," he said, and fog floated in front of his face.

He looked at the dry land in the thicket, his eyes focused to catch any movements in the dark shadows. Even the tiny activity of a darting bird or a falling leaf didn't escape scrutiny, but was carefully listened to and looked at, and eliminated as the source of the noise. Satisfied after a few motionless minutes, he stepped carefully toward the edge of the thicket, pulling the canoe, which occasionally scrubbed against a tree trunk.

Through the hanging vines and trunk of trees, he could see the huge oak. The location he'd left the giant buck. From what he could figure by judging the shortened distance between the water and the tree, in less than an hour the entire island would be covered in water above his knees. The oncoming overflow would run every air-breathing animal off the island, except for those that dwelled in the trees.

He stepped toward dry land, feeling his way with his boots still perplexed about the strange noise he'd heard.

Now that some time had passed, he began to wonder if the water itself had made the noise. He scratched his chin and shifted his camouflage clothing with one hand, then lowered both hands to his task as his eyes scanned the swamp thicket for movement.

Then it came again, a soft sob in the air.

"What the hell *is* that?"

He stopped. Forcing his ears to ignore the expected sounds and listen for the unusual. Small tree limbs, stick-jams and tree trunks seemed to push against the fast water, making sounds like wind chimes. But those sounds, he recognized. He scanned the dark thicket again, but saw nothing surprising.

As he stepped forward he glanced back to watch the canoe that floated behind him. The canoe got wedged between trees again. He stopped to free it and moved on.

The horizon was growing over the orange sun; in the west, the bright planet Venus looked like it was going down in the western sky too. The environment was still, as if holding its breath. Its blood was water flowing strong like Melvin's.

Thirty minutes it'll be dark. But that's okay, 'cause the moon's gonna be bright tonight.

He heard owls dueling in the distance. He looked to his right and three weary wood ducks floated in the fast current.

Just then, snarls then a dog fight.

That's coyotes ...

Now that he had identified the sound, he wedged the canoe between two trees and remained as still as he could, his heart pumping harder. He scanned the vicinity of the thicket for movement, and let out a breath when he saw nothing.

The noise came again. This time he heard the sound clearly and knew its direction.

Melvin was a half a football field above the spot where the buck was. He looked at the canoe. It was still firmly wedged between trees, and he left it there so he could move faster toward the buck. Grabbing the paddle, he started toward the dry land at the edge of the thicket.

Not enough time, he thought. But he could make better

time once he reached solid ground.

He pushed his legs forward, driving them, first one leg, then the other, splashing, pushing, splashing cold water up, pushing his legs forward, forward, then another leg, splashing, stumbling and balancing, forcing his way onward.

He was breathing hard, but he didn't care how hard he was breathing. All he knew was that he'd heard coyotes nearby, and it was still about thirty yards to the buck once he reached land.

When the water became shallow he took long strides, then longer, splashing, half-stumbling, half-running.

Just as he reached dry land, his foot got tangled in some vines and he fell forward, hitting the ground with a thud. Leaves and mud splashed away from the spot where he landed. He sprung to his feet and quickly washed his hands in the water.

Then he grabbed up the paddle and walked in long strides, guided by the sounds. He avoided the sticks and limbs on the ground, and the dogged limbs sprouting out from the brush and the rotting tree trunks lying on top of the leaves and thick mud.

Alongside the thicket now, the sounds were clearer, and closer. They would become quieter for a moment, then louder. Soon he was able to hear the shrill gurgling, the growling: spine-chilling sounds. Guided by them, he moved in the thick brush of briars and saplings where he could see the buck—*his* buck—battling a pack of coyotes. In that split-second, Melvin counted seven of them.

One ran in and took a bite of the buck's hindquarter. The buck reared up, pulling the oak sapling down on top of its hip, wielding its antlers, slashing at anything that moved. But as Melvin watched the coyote back away, the buck collapsed.

Before the first animal retreated, another coyote raced in to grab the buck by its snout. The buck pinned this one, twisting and grinding its antlers into the coyote's belly.

Mud and leaves exploded off the ground. The coyote squealed and got loose, then ran with its gray, bushy tail tucked between its legs a short distance. It stopped and licked itself, then rushed back for more.

As though that coyote's actions gave the rest permission, all the coyotes were on the buck's back in a flash, chewing and snapping at its hide, twisting their heads, ripping and tearing with their jaws and teeth, attempting to eat the buck alive.

One coyote worked its way beneath the buck's body and was biting its belly. The buck desperately tried to gore it, but the big antlers were only tossing up clods of mud and leaves.

Then two big coyotes got into a violent quarrel, bouncing and rolling around on the ground like one ball of fur. Another coyote lifted its broad head and stared with black eyes at Melvin.

Melvin came out of his disbelieving state. He removed

his pistol from his pocket and exploded out of the thicket with his paddle, yelling *"Git, Git, Git-outta here."*

The coyotes scattered like a flushed covey of quail. When they were ten or fifteen yards away, four or five of them stopped and turned, looking back at the old man. The other coyotes bounced a couple of times, then vanished in the thicket. But these started circling, growling low, led by one coyote that was bigger than the others.

Melvin rushed to position himself behind the buck, then slung his boat paddle at a big alpha male, yelling, "Git."

The big coyote bowed up and snarled, curling its lips at him. Enraged, Melvin fired his pistol once, then twice.

The big coyote chased its bushy tail in a frenzied spin, like it was performing a ceremonial dance circling a scorching fire. The coyote stopped mid-spin and toppled over like a bronze stature.

The buck reared up at the gunshots, pulling on the nylon rope that anchored him to the oak sapling. The sapling had held, but things didn't look good; the buck's power had loosened the small tree's roots from the soft earth.

Melvin walked to where the paddle lay and picked it up, then watched another coyote slipping in the thickets. He fired again, and the coyote disappeared into the dark undergrowth.

Chapter 17

Melvin looked at the wild in the buck's eyes as it stood on its front two legs. Its butt shook, then trembled, and collapsed back to the ground. It strained to come up again, but down it fell in the mud and soaked leaves. Holes and pits were dug in the soft ground where the buck made its gallant stand against the coyotes.

Gasping, Melvin scanned the thickets and saw one of the coyotes standing, ears perked, searching for a weakness, ready to rush in for the kill.

Melvin glanced back at the buck, then back to where the coyote was originally standing. That part of the thicket was empty now. He returned his attention to the buck's eyes and saw a wounded, dangerous animal—just as dangerous as a desperate man.

At least an animal is predictable, he thought, breathing too hard to laugh.

From where he stood, Melvin saw where the coyotes had torn away a piece of hide the size of a dinner plate on the buck's hindquarters. Not just hide, but also a section of lean meat was exposed.

Seeing this saddened him, and he muttered a curse under his breath. The last thing he wanted was for the buck to suffer like those who'd been hit by a vehicle, then left to bloat and rot beside the road. He'd seen what a vehicle could do to a deer: bust them up on the inside, leaving them to run off and suffer before they died.

He knew what had to be done, and done quickly. He didn't want the buck to be terrorized or to suffer any longer.

The buck rose up when Melvin walked to within ten steps, but not in a challenge. *More like defeat*, Melvin thought. Without hesitation, he fired at its neck once, then twice.

At the exact moment he fired the second time, the giant buck's head blew to the side and when it did the buck reared up, pulling forward on its front legs, bulling its way toward the water, digging, and its hooves churning the mud. It pulled with its powerful front shoulders and strained with its two front legs. With a wet ripping noise, the small tree pulled out of the wet earth exposing tangled roots.

The buck took off. It dragged its butt and hindquarters like it walked on shaky stilts. It headed straight for the rising water.

Melvin knew deer were strong swimmers, but the buck was badly wounded. If Mossback made it that far, he'd get into the strong current and sink like a rock. Once he sunk, he'd be swept away and lost forever. And Melvin was out of bullets. At last, he knew what he'd forgotten back at the camp house, more bullets.

Melvin couldn't figure out how the buck was still alive anyway. He knew he'd hit the buck with at least one shot, because he saw its neck jerk to the right. But now, he didn't see where the round hit.

Awed and stunned, he watched the buck moving for the water. He thought if he could knock the buck down and keep it down it would die.

Couldn't be much different from what he'd done as a cowboy while bulldogging cows. Sure, he was older, but the buck was hurt, and weaker than any cow he ever subdued as a young man. With no more hesitation, Melvin took off after the buck.

He ran up to the monster's left side and, with his right shoulder, shoved it off its front legs. The buck hit the ground.

Melvin lost his balance and stumbled. He shot his arms out in front of his body to soften the impact as he walloped the ground chest first, and slid about three feet in the mud and leaves.

Just as quick, Mossback was up and digging in the mud, pulling its body toward the water.

Melvin got up on one knee and regained his balance. Half-stumbling, he ran up to the buck's left front shoulder, put his left forearm against the curve of the huge left beam and reached over and grabbed the antler's right beam with his right hand. Then he tossed his right leg over the buck's back.

He applied his strength and pulled back on the right beam. As he did, a small red cord of blood ejected from the buck's neck onto Melvin's chest.

They slammed the soggy earth together, and clods of mud and leaves and small deadwood blew up from the impact.

The great buck never stopped moving as it whipped its antlers around and dug frantically sideways in the mud with its front legs.

As it slashed its antlers side to side, they struck Melvin in the forehead, stunning him for a moment and laying open a three-inch gash above his right eye. Blood blurred his vision for a moment, but he held on.

The buck's frothing jaws opened wide in a silent scream, and its still-powerful lungs forced open the buck's nostrils. Pink, bubbling foam formed on its nose. The heavier it breathed, the faster the foam ballooned like rose soapsuds.

Melvin's strength was no match for the buck's power but he didn't let go the antlers. He kept a firm grip when up the buck came, pulling Melvin, digging toward the water.

Its hooves sunk deeper in the mud as it went, dragging the old man, half-walking, half-stumbling behind it. Melvin felt like he was trying to wrestle a raging bull. He felt the animal's strength.

He shifted his right hand higher on the main beam to get a better grip. With his left forearm behind the main beam, he jerked the buck's right antler hard to the inside again.

They both crashed onto the ground; mud and soaking-wet leaves blew up into the frigid air.

Hot blood from the buck's neck spattered Melvin's face and eyes, blurring his vision for a moment. The buck thrashed, jerked and pulled its antlers, attempting to wrench Melvin's grip away, but the old man held on as the buck reared up and back.

He managed to reach his right forearm around the great buck's huge neck, and pulled back hard on its windpipe.

To protect his face from the whipping antlers, he moved his left forearm higher on the main curve on the buck's beam. Then, with his right forearm, he pulled back on the buck's throat with all his might.

Blood shot out from the buck's nose as it reared straight up on its front two legs, lifting the old man off the ground. Then, like a bass trying to toss a plug, the buck shook its head frantically and violently trying to dislodge Melvin from its back. The large brown eyes with a tint of green looked straight into Melvin's, startling him, but he held on and leaned back with all his might, determined to not let go.

The buck fell over on its left side, dislodging Melvin's grip from around its throat.

Just as quickly, the great buck was on its front two legs and heading toward the water, still dragging the oak sapling behind it.

Melvin was up, never pausing to catch his breath, and

quickstepped over the buck's back as its front legs were churning and sinking deeper in the mud. With his left forearm against the main beam, he gripped the buck's right beam and leaned with his weight to his left, sure that would bring the buck down.

Instead, the buck reared straight back and fell on top of Melvin. There was no time for Melvin to even scream as he landed on his back with a *whump* in the mud.

The buck was up, stabbing at him with its front hooves and trying to gore him with its antlers. The antlers whipped, jerked, and slashed side to side, then pushed down on Melvin's stomach, pinning him, grinding, grinding hard, harder, twisting its antlers, driving Melvin's back into the mud, sliding him backward.

All the time, the buck's huge, dark eyes were wide in a searing wildness Melvin had never seen before. Foaming red blood sprouted quickly on the buck's nostrils, spraying tiny bubbles that spotted Melvin's face and clothes.

Melvin held up his hands and forearms, attempting to fight off the stabbing hooves; at the same time, he moved his head like a prizefighter trying to avoid a blow to his head.

Involuntarily he yelled out, screaming, kicking at anything he could with his boots. He felt something tear in his stomach as the buck's hooves punched his midsection. Even so, he felt little pain; his insulated suit and chest waders were a shield against the blows. But the hooves were hitting Melvin like a boxer's body shots, nearly knocking the wind out of his lungs. Red foam grew on the buck's snout with each hard exhale, and the blood sprinkled Melvin's face.

He wasn't going to give up. He couldn't give up. The Army had taught him to never give up. *Never quit, you must fight and kill to survive.*

Melvin kept kicking with his legs. When he felt them grow heavy, a sense of impending doom caused him to breathe heavier, fight more frenziedly, like the buck.

His only chance was to get under the buck where the buck couldn't gore him or hit him with his hooves. If he could do that, he'd have perhaps two seconds to turn the battle to his advantage. Desperation gave him strength.

Shielding himself as best he could from the constant blows, he maneuvered on his back until he was beneath the buck's body, then grabbed for its left front leg—the one that, at the moment, was partially sunk into the mud. After several attempts, he grabbed onto the leg, put his boot at the base of the buck's neck and flipped the buck over onto its right side.

Just as fast the buck was up, stabbing with its hooves and slicing with its antlers. Its white belly looked like soft, muddy cotton.

Melvin yelled in desperation, crawling on his back, using his elbows and boot heels, kicking at the front hooves stabbing at his legs. The buck's massive antlers kept slicing stabbing, trying to pin Melvin again.

Without thinking, he yelled out, then grabbed mud and leaves in his right hand and tossed it in the direction of the buck's antlers.

Instantly, it wheeled away and charged toward the water. Its powerful shoulders rippled with muscles as it pulled forward dragging the oak sapling.

Melvin felt numbness above his right eye. The vision in that eye was still blurred, but he didn't know why. From his good eye, Melvin saw the great buck's legs dig down deep in the mud and its hooves churn forward toward the oncoming water. The buck was almost there.

Melvin struggled to his feet, holding his right side. Breathing heavy, he didn't know if he was beat. All he knew was if the buck got to the water, it would be lost. He wasn't going to abandon the fight or give up. Instinct told him it would be a fight to the death. That was all right. If he died, he would die fighting a great buck.

But the buck was tiring, getting slower in the mud. Melvin still had a chance. Holding his right side, blood dripping from the gash above his eye, breathing heavy, Melvin sprinted after Mossback.

Chapter 18

Growling, Melvin ran up to the buck, put his left forearm against the curved left beam, gripped the right beam with his right hand and tossed his right leg over the buck's back. He shifted his weight and twisted the buck's neck; its blood spewed onto his chest and they slammed into the mud and leaves next to the swift-running stream.

As they flounced and fought in the mud, Melvin could tell the buck neared exhaustion. The realization gave him enough strength to tighten his grip on the beams.

The buck's eyes were wide, wild and black with that tint of green. Its mouth was wide-open, and it was choking on its blood.

Melvin was nearly out of breath, but didn't realize it. He didn't feel the pain in his chest or the tearing in his stomach. He didn't feel the warm blood coming from his mouth, from the gash above his eye or from his nose.

The deep bone-bruise in his thigh didn't affect him. He felt nothing but the weight on his legs and the sweet smell of the buck's blood on his face, and the urgency of keeping the buck out of the knee-deep water.

If the buck got to the water, he'd be out of time, defeated. If it got as far as the main slough, it would sink and be swept away by the fast-moving current.

Just then, Mossback pulled loose from Melvin's grip and

was up and stabbing the water with its front legs, splashing deeper until its hooves sunk to a point well above its knee-joint. The buck kept looking back at the old man, kept bulling forward. Each step, the great buck was finding it difficult to remove its legs from the sucking mud.

Melvin saw it was tiring. He waded into the freezing water and caught up with the buck as it dropped down from exhaustion.

At Melvin's touch, the great buck reared up and started digging forward.

Melvin made a desperate lunge and reached around the buck's neck. Again he placed his left forearm against the left curve of the slashing rack, and then he grabbed the main spike with his left hand. With his right forearm around the buck's windpipe, he pulled back hard and quickly shifted his weight to his left.

His motion made them both go down into the gray-brown water, and it blew up around them.

When the buck fell, Melvin's left leg was pinned beneath its body, but he managed to keep his head above water.

The buck's head went under, but came up quick.

Melvin placed his right forearm beneath its throat and locked his legs tight around its body, then squeezed his legs and pulled back. Like a lion he dug in, pulling with all his strength. Grinding his teeth, he saw serrated limbs of gray in his vision. He wasn't going to let go this time.

He tried to hold the buck's snout beneath the water, but the buck still had too much strength. Next, he worked his left forearm around the main beam of the antlers again and grabbed hold of the left spike that rose up from the antlers' main frame.

His right forearm went on the inside of the main beam, and he locked his hands on the buck's head just behind the antlers. Holding tight, he pushed his head through the antlers onto the buck's forehead and applied his weight to the buck's head, forcing its scooped-out snout into the water.

The buck's wide head forced up and it gasped for air, but Melvin held his grip. He used his weight to force its muzzle under water. It was easier this time, but he, too, was tiring.

When the buck came up again, Melvin pushed its muzzle back under. But this time, the buck pushed up suddenly and flipped over on top of him.

The buck's legs were straight up now, with Melvin's legs still locked around its body. Melvin's head went under the water. He held his breath and felt his head being pushed down in the mud and leaves.

The buck lay on top of him; all it had to do was stay there to finish Melvin off. But it rolled off him and attempted to stand, with its enemy holding onto its antlers.

Melvin managed to get his face barely out of water and he gulped, gulped for air.

The buck's front legs went deep into the sucking mud; Melvin's legs remained locked around its belly. The buck's strength was waning, but so was Melvin's.

The buck's mouth was wide open as if calling out and the foam coming from its injured snout was no longer pink, but red.

Melvin maneuvered around on the buck's antlers again. This time he put his chest between the spikes of the antlers and pushed down on top of its muzzle with all his weight.

The buck violently tried to rear up, but its front legs were buried too deep and it wasn't strong enough anymore. This gave Melvin his first real hope that he might survive.

He placed his forearm behind its antlers and held its muzzle in the water with his weight.

The buck attempted to rear up again, but it barely managed to raise its snout.

Melvin pushed down more, forcing the muzzle deeper into the water that was now above Melvin's knees.

Up again the buck pushed, spurting blood from its nostrils, vomiting blood and water from its gaping jaws.

Again, Melvin pushed down. The buck still struggled to raise its head above the murky water. Melvin countered with all his weight and strength, which was so much less than before, he panicked and almost let go of the buck.

Then he no longer saw the buck, but the blonde hair and desperate blue eyes of a German soldier, struggling with cheeks full of air, trying to push up, trying desperately to get air as Melvin and he were locked in hand-to-hand combat. The soldier tried to raise his head and Melvin pushed back, frantically trying to drown the soldier, not wanting to hear the pleading voice again.

With all the strength he could summon, fighting the pain in his side, Melvin pushed against the soldier's strength, against the soldier's attempts to raise his head out of the water. Each time the soldier gasped, *"Bitte, bitte, nicht, bitte, bitte, nicht,"*

Melvin swore and applied his weight again. He felt his own strength starting to drain, and the words, in an echo, an unexecuted whispering from the past: *"Never give up. You're an American fighting man, you gotta be the best! Never give up, never, never give up..."*

The soldier attempted to rise, but his legs were buried too deep in the swamp's mud. Swearing, Melvin applied all his strength to the soldier's throat, at the same time pushing the face beneath the water.

The soldier made another, gallant attempt, fighting to raise his head from beneath the water, straining against Melvin's weight. Up the soldier came, vomiting blood. Melvin cursed and applied his youthful strength and weight to the soldier's head.

At last, Melvin felt the life leaking out from the soldier's jerking body. Just to be sure, he held the German's head beneath the muddy water for another five minutes. He felt the still-warm and twitching muscles jerk, but felt nothing else. Nothing except a grim rage, combined with a fear he'd only known once before. Covered in blood, his adversary's and his own, he remembered.

Blocked out of his mind for decades, his memory returned of that fearful life-and-death struggle in a muddy shell hole on the battlefield in France in 1918. Only the strong survived that day, and the words *please, please don't!* In German haunted him to this day.

Melvin couldn't feel his legs, toes or fingers. He felt no fear, no pain and no cold. He didn't breathe or think, or wonder about anything.

Suddenly he was hurting, but not from his chest, or from his stomach, or from the cold. He scarcely moved and hardly breathed; he remained that way, in the mud and leaf-choked water, for uncountable minutes.

After a time, he released the antlers and his hand dropped, inert, into the water. He was confused, unsure what to do, the same way he'd felt right after taking the German soldier's life.

He knew he had to move right away, or he wouldn't make it. But he was too comfortable and relaxed to move, didn't feel the creeping-slow, warm death entering his body.

It terrified him to think about dying alone in the swamps on top of the monster buck with the water rising. He knew he had to recover quickly. *We'll never be found. No one will ever know I finally got the ghost-buck.*

That thought, and that thought alone saved him. He started working his legs free from beneath the buck's body. Once his feet released from the mud with a soft sucking feeling, he tried to stand several times, but his legs didn't want to work right. He hated the helplessness. The renewed cold rushing through the soaked, heavy clothing didn't faze him, but not being able to move his legs to stand was shameful.

He fought the humiliation by crawling on hands and knees through the knee-deep water. As he shoved his hands forward, the gash above his eye bled and burned. By the time he reached the bank, he was unable to recall a time he was so exhausted.

After pulling his soaked, muddy body out of the water, he dragged himself to a small tree. He rolled over, leaned his back against the tree and spread out his legs. Each time he took a breath, he felt pain in his chest. His right arm tingled and his fingers felt numb. He twisted his arm several times.

Must 'a pulled a nerve.

As he leaned against the tree in the mud and leaves, he breathed hard and stared at the huge antlers protruding from Mossback's head. After a moment he said, "It's over," just as he had forty-six years before.

He felt something dripping in his throat; his croupy-sounding cough produced blood. He spat it out, then wiped his face and nose on his sleeves, smearing mud and blood over his face when he did. He felt a swelling the size of a plum, a tightening knot on his forehead. When he reached up to touch it, he drew back a bloody, muddy finger. He knew it was a deep gash, because he'd put his finger in the wound, and, as he probed, he was sure he touched his own skull.

After about five minutes, he struggled to his feet with the help of the little tree. He was exceptionally strong for his age, but the weather and the fight had drained him. Keeping busy, moving around—getting the blood to flow was the key to him surviving, and he knew it.

When he managed to regain his balance, he felt a digging pain in his stomach. He leaned against the tree a moment, holding his side, and took a deep breath.

He felt something the size of a goose egg on his right side, just under the muscle below the ribcage. He didn't want to think about it now. If he did, the rising water might take Mossback away from him, and that was unacceptable. After a few minutes, he summoned enough strength to wade out to the buck.

He paused a moment and looked at the gigantic rack, then gripped the antlers with both hands and leaned back, pulling the buck through the muddy water. The buck's front legs were still buried in the mud, and he had to twist the antlers to jar the body loose.

Melvin had seen many floods, but was surprised at how fast the water was rising. It took some doing, but he got the buck's head back onto dry land. As soon as he dragged the deer partially out of the water, he let the rack drop and left it there.

He looked across the slough. In the moonlight, he could see trunks of trees trapping deadwood in the rising water. Further in the distance, he saw other tree trunks starting to merge into one. He was sure the canoe hadn't drifted off, though; even in his panic, habit made him wedge it tight between the two trees.

Nausea overcame him. He leaned his head down as if to vomit, but only coughed up blood mixed with saliva when he spit.

I'll worry later. I gotta get the canoe. Still so much to do.

He walked upstream toward the spot where he'd left the canoe lodged between trees. Occasionally, he would dodge a tree limb by moving his head.

His camouflage suit was soaked and bulky, and the chest waders underneath had taken on water, making his journey slow. He stopped and coughed several times, and the pain was like a knife now.

When he saw the canoe in the spot he left it, he smiled. But he knew he had to move faster, before the serious water from the Alabama River flooded in. If he didn't hurry, that current would make his trip along the slough iffy. And dark was closing in.

Wish Chad was here.

As soon as he recovered, he got the canoe undone from the trees and started wading back to the spot he'd left the buck, steering the canoe as he went along.

When he reached the spot, he pulled the canoe alongside the buck, lifted the canoe up and leaned it against the tree.

He dragged the buck away from the water and close to the canoe, but not too close. There was still something he had to do before he could load the buck for its journey to the camp house.

With a grim face, he unzipped his coveralls and removed the scabbard from the pouch in his chest waders. He unsnapped his scabbard and removed the knife, then flipped open the sharp blade and straddled the buck.

When he slit open the belly, the cavity gave off steam and a sharp, pungent odor. He cut away the guts with care, and cut the cheesecloth-looking membrane that separated the guts from the lungs and heart.

Fresh blood from the gash over his right eye dripped into the cavity and mixed with the buck's blood. He reached with his two hands far into the cavity and felt for the connection of the heart and lungs, then cut them away with the buck's windpipe. He pulled out the mechanics, a term he used for the heart and lungs, left them in the pile on the ground, then rolled the buck on its belly so the cavity would drain the clumps of red jelly inside. As he worked, he wondered if a hunter is more benevolent than nature after all.

While waiting for the blood to drain, Melvin looked at the round, gaping wound on the buck's hip left by the coyotes. Then he inspected the deep punch-wound made by the flint arrowhead. There was no sign of the flint point, and he was disappointed.

Out of curiosity, he grabbed the gut pile and lugged it about ten yards away, then slit open the plump, grayish purple stomach to see what the deer had been eating. He found only water oak acorns, specks of green and a yellowish, watery pulp.

When Melvin raised his eyes, he saw his ground stand, and decided to get his pack and the paddle. Water would cover the stand in a couple of hours; no need to leave the knapsack to be washed away and lost.

He went back to the edge of the water and washed his hands, then shuffled to the stand, and then to the spot he thought he'd dropped the paddle. He was pleased to discover it, but his smile faded when he saw the spot where the buck was originally tied. The spot looked like a hog had wallowed it out, and blood and deer hair littered the entire area. He stood in stone silence for a minute, just staring, then turned to go back to the canoe.

Once there, instead of moving toward the canoe, he sat down and leaned his back against a tree. He didn't think and no thoughts came to him at first; he stared into the darkening sky, his face a blank. After a while, he was able to take stock. He breathing was normal now, not too heavy. The pain had eased some, too. No new pains anywhere. He listened, and the only thing he heard was the running water and an occasional owl in the distance.

But the dark was coming thicker now. It got dark first in the swamps. The ridge and tree canopy made sure of it. He knew he should get going. Even with the moonlight, it would be full dark in ten minutes or less. On the other hand, he knew a minute or two of rest would benefit him for his journey out of the swamps.

Out of nowhere came a sound, a noise that didn't fit. It was so near he froze. Hardly had he felt chills than he felt eyes pressing on his back. He'd never heard the sound before, but he knew what it was from hearing others talk about it. He held his breath.

Yeah, they talk about it. And they fret about it, too. It's the thing hunters think about walking into the swamps to hunt before daylight. The thing that haunts and stalks the mind when coming out from the swamps after dark. When a panther's on the prowl, the hunter's the prey.

Melvin didn't move, because he felt the presence right behind him. *Too close.* The hair on his neck spiked when the sound came again, the noise that didn't fit.

He took a deep slow breath, and slowly craned his head to peek behind the tree trunk. The first thing he saw were big yellow eyes, a broad black head, then sleek black fur, and his terror climbed.

Ten yards away, a swamp panther with a tail as long as a gun barrel was staring back at Melvin. A panther. The thing that would leap from a tree and attack a man, biting and holding a man behind the neck with its jaw, digging into the man's back with its claws. And it was almost on top of him.

The eighty-pound panther was on the gut pile, and when it saw Melvin move, it hunkered down with a spit. The low, gurgling growl seemed to go on forever, a growl that would send any man's blood pressure through the roof. The big animal was ready to defend the gut pile.

Keeping its eyes on Melvin, the panther lay with its legs along both sides of the guts. It buried its fangs into the deer's liver, bit fast, tearing with its spike-filled jaw. Its yellow eyes never left Melvin's, and the bodyguards of Melvin's courage, the ones who'd kept him alive so far, froze.

Through all his years in the swamps and forests, he'd never seen a panther or a wildcat. A few bobcats, but this wasn't a bobcat. No, this was a hunter's worst nightmare: a big panther known by legend to attack and kill humans. A tale told by Creek Indians about a spirit that wails in the dark like a squaw. A jewel so rare, so rarely seen, not even an artist could capture or frame the magnificence Melvin saw before him now.

So that's what's been stalking me at night. Not the buck. A black panther. That's what killed my animals. A panther.

After a few moments, the cat let its prize drop; then it bared its fangs. Growling, it rose up slow and took one soft step toward Melvin.

Melvin didn't move again; he had no strength left to battle, wasn't even sure if he *could* fight a black panther. Didn't think any human could barehanded. And he'd left the knife next to the gut pile.

The panther's long black tail was even with its back when it gave another low, soft growl, then slowly stepped forward, slowly forward, its body hunkered down, its muscles full of energy as if preparing to stalk and kill a prey.

Cut, half-blind from the bleeding above his eye, nearing collapse, Melvin was no match, and he knew it.

After an eternity, the panther returned to the gut pile, grabbed the guts with its jaw and bit fast several times, keeping its big yellow eyes on Melvin. Without warning, it turned and started walking off, rocking from side to side with the weight of the guts dragging between its powerful legs. In moments, the big panther merged with the dark.

Chapter 19

Absent of leaves, the frozen bare limbs gave a grisly appearance to the swamps. Vines that looked like ropes in the daylight now looked like exposed dark blood vessels nursing a tree. Powerful water made chilling sounds in the rapids. Where the water was tranquil, a solid, ash-colored bedspread of leaves, twigs and vines lay lifeless on the surface.

In the distance, owls dueled and quarreled over territory, and a nightingale sobbed in loneliness. In the purple sky, stars proliferated and the moon gave the swamps an eerie glow.

With the dark encroaching, menacing sounds tiptoed, in the frigid air. The swamps seemed jumpy. Melvin wondered if the panther was real or an illusion; the stare between them happened so fast.

With another slow turn of his head, he scanned the spot where the guts had been. Steam still rose, but the guts were gone.

The sight invigorated him, stirred his imagination, and filled him with a thrill—a thrill craved by a hunter, an insurance policy given to the pure hunter, an excitement derived from the dangers in the hunt. Once he tasted the thrill, the hunter wanted more and more. He coveted it, obsessed about it. There was no satisfying it; he only wanted the stakes higher and higher.

It's the one thing true hunters have in common, he thought in that moment of clarity, *the thrill in the kill. Without that, hunting would be as dull as a gallon of water.*

Melvin wondered if that thrill, that craving, was nature's reward, or its punishment.

He struggled to his feet, using the tree as a pole to pull himself up. After he regained his balance, he started to work on positioning the canoe. He inspected the wood patch on the bottom and inside of the canoe, thinking how, together, the two pieces of wood worked well.

Will *work well. Have to.*

The canoe made thumping noises as he moved it around. The noises were intentional, to spook any curious animal that might be coming off the island because of the flooding water. The noise gave him assurance; the work occupied his mind and kept him concentrating on his task.

While he worked, he listened for unusual sounds, and occasionally glanced up and surveyed his surroundings for any movement in the moonlit dark.

He knew he was tired and growing weak . . . in no condition for a quarrel. He wasn't as worried about the panther—it was probably still feeding on what it had taken—but about the pack of coyotes that might come back around to investigate the scent of the kill.

The pain limited his speed. Taking a deep breath forced him to stand straight and hold his side. He wondered if his clothes were restricting his breathing, so he fumbled with the zipper and unzipped the coveralls to his waist.

The deep gash over his right eye had clotted, and his vision was clear now, but when he bent down for the boat paddle, he felt as if someone had shoved an ice pick into his side.

The pain made him straighten to an almost-standing position. He remained that way, catching his breath, holding his side with his right hand, willing the pain away, *knowing* the pain would go away. Like a wounded boxer, he paced slowly in the sucking mud and soggy leaves to regain his strength.

A misty, low fog had begun to move in from the rising water. With every passing minute, he imagined something was moving in the dark fifty yards away, then twenty-five.

A lemon rose in his stomach when he thought he saw something move from behind one tree trunk to another in the moon's glow.

It was like the sensation he'd got in France during the war, when he felt a sniper had his head in the gun sights. Again, he sensed the wisp of a bullet and felt heat on the end of his tongue.

He remembered his dream that came, off and on, when he was especially tired. The nightmare that made him sweat and wake up with a sudden jerk. He was going through the muddy war trenches in France. Arms protruded out of the bank, trying to grab him as he approached a small clearing.

The knee-high grass in the clearing was matted down

in spots where bloated soldiers lay, their eyes open, mouths wide with silent screams. And always the same soldier kneeling as if to pray, with an astonished look in his eyes, eyes that had a fist-sized gob of macaroni dangling by a single spaghetti cord that hung down his forehead. A spaghetti cord that always snapped, dropping the goo to the ground as Melvin watched. Then snakes would leap out of the grass and strike Melvin's legs, striking, striking until he woke up in a sweat. It was a haunting he feared, at times, when he went to sleep. He thought he would surely have it tonight.

His coveralls made a crackling noise as he moved about. When he reached down and rubbed his hand across them, he was surprised at how stiff they felt. He looked down and saw tiny threads of ice in the creases. But he wasn't cold. His fingers felt thick, and were hard to bend, but he didn't feel any soreness in them. Yet he knew he had to get going or he would soon freeze.

Carefully, to avoid straining too much, he pulled the buck onto the edge of the canoe's frame, and positioned the deer on the inside of the canoe as far as he could. With great effort, he shoved the canoe out from the tree, and, when the canoe landed on the mud and leaves, the buck was nearly in.

After he positioned the buck on its side, he moved the wide antlers until they faced the bow of the canoe. They stuck up and off the sides of the bow. The buck's body covered the plywood patch he'd made, and he was glad.

As he shifted the antlers he felt a tightening in his thigh, like a Charlie horse, but after a few moments, the tightening went away. He didn't feel as much pain as before, but knew he would feel more pain soon enough.

Like a football player the day after a game. He grinned at the comparison.

When he checked his flashlight, its beam was dim. The moon was bright, but he kept the flashlight on anyway and slid it into his pocket, with the weak shaft of light facing up to give a bit of extra illumination in front of him.

Tentatively, he touched the sore spot at his midsection and felt, through his clothing, the deep, goose-egg-sized swelling. He pressed it and felt nothing, but heard a sound under his skin.

He'd felt no pain when he was standing, but the noise when he applied pressure was like a soft burst of static. The sound was enough to remove the secure feeling he had.

He paused to catch his breath and thought how the swelling might be a severely strained muscle, not a tear or a hernia. He hoped it wasn't a hernia, because that operation was painful and took a long time to heal. He dreaded the prospect of an operation, couldn't think of anything worse. Except maybe freezing to death. "What a choice," he muttered, and his chuckle was grim.

Standing in the water now, he bent down, grasped the canoe's bow and leaned back with all his weight, jarring the canoe from the sucking mud. Inch by inch he leaned back, drawing the canoe into the water.

He felt his boots sinking in the mud and noticed how his legs felt like lead weights at times. Instead of thinking about that, he forced himself to listen to the water splashing and whirling as he pulled on the canoe.

The fog boiled up around him with each step on the water's surface, making it difficult for him to judge distance. Soft chimes made by water trickling over the driftwood trapped behind trees were the only sounds he could use to fathom his bearing and direction.

He could still see the tree line, though, and a path cut out in the towering trees—a wide clearing, like a highway in the moonlit skyline where the slough flowed. Seeing that, he knew where he was, and where he was headed.

After a few minutes, he managed to pull the canoe into knee-deep water. He got into the canoe safely, grabbed the paddle, knelt down as if to pray, then shoved the paddle in the mud and pushed the canoe, propelling it slowly forward.

As he expected, he felt a smothering heat in his thighs and calf muscles for a minute before the discomfort disappeared. Bracing for the next wave of it, he shoved with the paddle and the canoe glided forward like a spirit gliding on the dense fog, floating without a sound.

In between strokes, Melvin considered his situation. The buck's body weight against it might hold the inner patch. But his weight and the buck's weight put the rim of the canoe six, maybe eight inches above the water. He believed he'd be all right as long as he kept away from the fast-moving current, especially when he encountered the channel.

He knew he had to be extremely careful because the fog, rising higher now, was causing him problems in judging distance. Gone was the noise of water flowing over the beaver dam: what he would have otherwise used to judge where he was. The water had surely covered the dam, likely had destroyed it.

Once he got past the channel he could paddle into the flats, then wade down to Fannie Road with the canoe. For a while, he quarreled with himself about wading, because his legs already felt too heavy to travel the length of one football field from the channel to Fannie Road. Finally, he figured he would decide when he got there.

He pulled the paddle out and shoved it back deeper, bit by bit, pushing the canoe toward the channel. The water current's muscle worried him too.

He shifted the paddle to his right side, then back to his left, paddling without thinking, by instinct. Occasionally the fog seemed to boil again as the canoe glided forward.

He floated and drifted, dodging tree trunks with the canoe. In some spots, he could only inch the canoe forward with the paddle, being careful to avoid getting wedged between trees. An occasional vine would tangle in the buck's huge antlers, forcing him to stop paddling and creep forward far enough to untangle the vines. As he did, he worked hard to keep from rocking the canoe too much.

After a time he could only guess at, he felt the current starting to tug on the canoe, and sensed he was getting close to the channel. He shoved the paddle deep until he felt bottom, then pushed hard until the canoe shot forward.

The strong current moved the canoe downstream two or three feet for every foot forward he pushed. At one point, he poked the paddle into the water and pushed the paddle backwards, but stopped when he felt the familiar ice pick in his side.

He sensed danger, not from the pain, but he could tell the canoe was drifting faster downstream and he hadn't hit the channel yet. Or at least he didn't think he had because he could, at times, touch bottom with his paddle.

He expected the channel to be deeper than that. Knowing it might be his last chance for a while, he swiped at his forehead with his muddy sleeves, wincing when he encountered the swollen bridge of his nose, then his cheeks. Other than those two spots, he had no feeling in his face.

With his right hand on the top of the paddle and his left hand at its center, he took a deep breath, poked the paddle in the water and pushed back hard. With a swirling sound, the canoe slipped forward.

When the canoe's bow hit the current, the bow spun downstream, the canoe spun around midstream and backwards. Now the canoe was in the most powerful current so far. Finally, he was in the slough's channel.

Melvin felt the ice pick in his side and grimaced as he attempted to get across the channel, which had turned into a swift channel.

He poked the paddle into the water and used it as a rudder to slow and steer the canoe. After much effort, he stopped the canoe's spin and righted it on course, in a deep, slow whirlpool near the bank.

In places along the slough, trees leaned over it, and their large limbs stretched to the other side. Spanish moss hung with the appearance of dark ice, and vines dangled down the walls, forming fractures. He looked up. What stars he could see blinked, assuring him he wasn't traveling through a cave or cavern.

The feeling that something was lying in wait on one of those big limbs, ready to pounce, goaded his thoughts, kept him on guard, looking up at each muscle-bound limb that stretched across the narrow slough.

If he could keep the canoe drifting close to the tree line in the deep whirlpools, away from the current, he could make better time. Yet it was more dangerous than maneuvering in the slow-moving water in the flats. Finally, he decided he felt more secure close to the tree line, and chose to drift along the edge of the current down to Fannie Road.

The swollen slough's channel would make a sharp turn, like an elbow, before the mouth of the slough merged into Flat Creek. This was his main concern. That area had steep banks, but he knew the muddy water was well over the banks now.

But once he cleared the elbow, the channel straightened out into Flat Creek. He would be about the length of a football field away from Fannie Road, and he could paddle into the flats, get out of the canoe and pull the canoe the rest of the way to the road.

His unease grew every time he looked up at the tree limbs, and he didn't want to prolong his stay in the water any longer than he had to.

Now more used to the speed of the current, he started drifting down the channel, using the paddle as a rudder and occasionally paddling.

He tried to drift clear of obstacles. Now and again, he'd duck to go beneath an overhanging tree limb, or reach out to move vines, moss or limbs away. Occasionally, the buck's antlers would get caught in a branch and nearly spin the canoe around.

After going the distance of two football fields, Melvin was gaining confidence. He felt inflammation only when he strained a certain way. He believed that was a good sign.

Nothing was perfectly calm on the water. Strange, muscle-bound shadows flexed in the fog. Melvin had courage, and a strength that had surprised him more than once, but nothing spooked him more than the swamps did in the dark. In the past, he'd managed to dominate his dread with his thoughts, but not now. He had a bad feeling that wouldn't leave him alone.

As Melvin approached the elbow at the mouth of the slough, the canoe picked up speed. Keeping close to the edge of the bank, he steered with the paddle, slowing the canoe down. Then the current would start to push, and he'd straighten the canoe with the paddle, rudder-like.

Soon, he saw the quick turn at the mouth of the slough. He moved the paddle in the water to slow the canoe and braced, and then spun the canoe into the powerful Flat Creek current.

Once there, he had no time to congratulate himself. He was still drifting, but fast, too fast at times. He kept the canoe close to the bank, moving swiftly toward where he believed the bank was located.

Once, when the current slowed enough, he allowed himself to feel relief, and reached up to carefully wipe his runny nose with his sleeve. Everything seemed so colorless and dull at night, no color of life.

All you can do is to listen, he thought.

Looking toward Fannie Road, his peripheral vision caught a glimpse of a light. He looked at the light and the beam seemed horizontal. When he heard a truck horn blow a couple of times, he immediately recognized the signal.

Excited, Melvin reached into his pocket, took his flashlight out and directed the beam through the trees, toward the light on Fannie Road. He yelled out. A moment later, a truck horn answered his signal.

Squinting to see better, he flipped the flashlight beam on and off until he saw the light beam signal back once, twice, a third time.

A proud smile came to his lips and that combined with a rare pride at killing such an enormous buck with a longbow made his eyes gleam. And he felt deep relief.

Chad could help him load the big buck. Chad could witness the buck's size before they butchered it for meat. Chad could see the ghost-buck that was no ghost, the buck that had tormented him for years, and testify to its massive web rack.

Chad can bear witness to the buck being brought out in a canoe.

Moving along fast now, Melvin was close to where the bank had been before Flat Creek rushed over it. The entire flats were flooded in two to three feet of water. But Flat Creek's channel was at last twenty and thirty feet deep now, turbulent and dangerous like the Colorado River. He couldn't let his excitement override his caution.

After drifting about twenty yards, he heard sounds of rapids, but he couldn't remember anything like that on Flat Creek. He pointed the flashlight in that direction and didn't see a thing.

He shoved his paddle in the current to slow the canoe, preparing to maneuver it closer to the bank. Just then, he saw a dark, round-looking shape horizontal in the creek, and a pile of tree roots shaped like a dark plate coming toward him.

He knew immediately it was a big tree that had fallen into the creek. The tree trunk was catching anything that floated, and he was still moving too fast.

Frantically, he tried to paddle the canoe closer to the tree line, where the soft, boiling pools would make it easier to handle.

Despite his exertion, the current took the canoe faster downstream. Still pushing back with the paddle, he held his breath, helpless, and watched the dark tree trunk and logjam coming at the canoe fast, much too fast.

He jabbed the paddle in the water again and again, straining hard, splashing, swirling the water with his paddle. But he knew it was futile when he saw the buck's antlers tangle with the first item in the logjam—a mammoth, waterlogged tree limb.

The canoe spun out of control in the swirling current, and the water pushed against the canoe until it plowed through the deadwood and crashed sideways against the tree trunk.

When the canoe hit, the buck's weight shifted and the canoe took on a bucketful of muddy water. The current, combined with the weight in the canoe, caused it to rock against the tree trunk.

Each time it rocked, the canoe took on more water. On one of the current's thrusts, the buck's antlers broke loose from the tree branch. The weight shifted again, harder, and the canoe took a barrelful of water this time. The canoe was going under.

In a panic, Melvin grabbed one of the limbs attached to the fallen tree. He let go of the paddle, pulled himself up, quickly put his leg over it and straddled the limb.

The shift in weight caused the canoe to dip upstream against the current, taking in more water, and then the current forced the canoe back against the tree trunk with a *thump*.

The surging water then pushed on the bottom of the canoe until it dipped and water flooded in. The canoe went under, taking Mossback with it.

Chapter 20

Melvin watched the canoe and the monster buck vanish without a sound beneath the surface, just like something reached up and grabbed them from below. His heart lurched with the force of his disbelief.

I should'a paddled into the flats and waded out, he thought, miserable.

The erosion ditches and deep ravines might have caused him trouble, but he knew he could have paddled across them. He had no time to be angry with himself.

As Melvin sat straddling the great limb, he felt the entire tree quiver. The water and current were probably washing out the bank underneath.

He looked over the trunk, saw the big pile of frosty-looking roots gleaming in the moonlight, and guessed the water was only a few feet deep there. But the current was already working to dislodge it from the bank. He must move quickly; before long, the entire tree would be washed away, and him with it. If he fell into the freezing water, he wasn't sure he could make it back out.

His gash was stinging as he worked his way up the tree trunk toward the muddy root pile that sprung out from the base of the tree.

He didn't know exactly where the bank started, but he felt confident it was right at or near the roots. For now, at least. The roaring sound of oncoming, still-rising water told him to get away from the bank as fast as possible.

He had an unsettling feeling when the tree shook again, much harder this time, and even swayed a bit. Holding on to the slippery trunk as best he could, he lowered his boots into the water, further and further until he could feel the ground under his cold, aching feet and grasp the ball of roots with cold-numbed hands.

The water was slightly above his waist here, a good sign. But he had to get further toward dry land before it rose much more; already, he could feel his exhausted leg muscles want to give in to the current.

He started feeling his way, heading straight for the small double beacon of light on Fannie Road. He knew the flats well, knew where the erosion ditches came off the ridge, but he was far south of them now.

After he crisscrossed the flats, dodging trees and half-frozen, waterlogged vines for a hundred yards or more, he removed his flashlight and directed its beam in the direction of Fannie Road, flipping the on and off switch repeatedly.

He could see the road through the tree trunks now and slowly moved toward it, occasionally holding onto a tree with his sore hands as he continued putting one boot, then the other ahead of him in a stumbling half-drag, half-walk through the water, which was only thigh-deep now.

The moon had painted Fannie Road a light orange color, but Melvin still saw a fast-moving, dim light disappear, then reemerge behind tree trunks, then disappear and emerge again on the road. When the light got about even with him, it stopped and blinked in his direction. He saw the broken outline of a human silhouette behind it. He called out, and the beam of light blinked back.

He felt neither panic nor relief as he waded methodically toward Fannie Road. If he had to travel farther than that, it would have been a major chore, but he felt . . . satisfied.

Satisfied the hunt was about over. Satisfied he had survived Mossback's attack, the coyotes and the panther, the freezing cold. Sad that he'd lost the buck, but glad to be alive.

Weary, he looked up and watched the stars a moment. He felt no real pain, just a quick, deep-down ache in his heart for what might have been.

Holding on to an oak sapling, he glanced back over his shoulders in the direction of the lost buck and canoe. Then, in knee-deep water, Melvin pushed his exhausted body forward toward the road, as if in retreat from a lost war.

* * *

When Melvin was only about ten yards from Fannie Road, he saw Chad about to come into the water to aid him.

"No." he yelled out. "Don't come in, too cold. I'm all right." Hearing how weak his voice sounded frightened him.

Chad waited at the edge of the road, watching Melvin

wading slowly through the water. When Melvin's right boot hit dry land, Chad said, "Let me asking you this, what the Sam hell's going on with you, Uncle Melvin?"

"Oh, nothing much," Melvin said, glad that Chad couldn't yell loud at him, but feeling chastised just the same.

Melvin dragged the other foot onto dry land and felt relieved, but his legs felt like lead weights. He looked at Chad again, still looking serious and now puzzled, too.

Chad pointed his flashlight at Melvin's face, scowling when he saw the deep gash and Melvin's swollen cheek.

"What the hell took after *you*?"

"I'll be all right," Melvin said, and then he looked toward Flat Creek Bridge, about fifty yards down the road. Now, he understood why he couldn't see the bridge before. The strong moonlight revealed that it was about a foot below water.

"Wait here," Chad said, then jogged up the road, got into his truck and backed it up to where Melvin was standing, then went around to the passenger side of the truck and opened the door.

Melvin looked at his clothes, then at the interior of Chad's pride and joy. "I'm muddy. Dirty."

"Don't hand me that, get in."

Melvin thought Chad's harsh words were the sweetest he'd ever heard—standing beside the open truck door, he could already feel the heat blowing from the vents inside.

Chad helped Melvin into the cab, closed the door, got in the truck and gunned it up the road to the camp house. On the truck's dusty dashboard were a crumpled coffee cup, a pair of pliers, a screwdriver and several shotgun shells that rattled and bumped the windshield.

The cab was warm, and it felt good, but Chad's silence made Melvin shiver as Chad turned from Fannie Road onto the lane leading to the camp house. It was stone silence. All that could be heard over the rattling shotgun shells was the engine, and the heater running.

* * *

At the camp house, Chad got out, then went around to the passenger side and helped Melvin out of the cab. Together they walked to the bottom steps.

"I can handle it from here," Melvin said. Chad reluctantly stepped back and let his uncle take the lead.

Legs stiff, Melvin climbed the few steps and walked into the porch light's glow just as Chad came to stand beside him.

"My gawd, we gotta get you to a doctor," Chad said.

Melvin shook his head, fighting not to wince. "I'll be all right. Few bumps, a little sore. That's all."

"Bumps, hell! I'm looking at least a three-inch gash on your forehead opened like an axe sliced you. Your nose is all swelled up, and you look like somebody stabbed you in the jaw with a pencil! What the hell happened?"

Melvin sighed. "I'm telling ya, it's just a cut. I must 'a hit a tree branch when I fell in the water. Just help me out of this hunting gear." He tried to smile. "And put on the kettle. I could use a cup 'a strong coffee right about now."

Still not accepting his uncle's light tone, Chad rushed inside, and Melvin started unzipping his camouflage coveralls.

Chad returned to the porch and helped him remove the coveralls, then the chest waders. He saw the blood soaked through the overalls around Melvin's shoulders, onto his once-white cotton long johns, but waited until Melvin caught his breath to speak.

"Man," Chad said, unable to stop staring at the blood. "Uncle Melvin, we gotta get you to a doctor *right away*."

"Well, *I* gotta get some coffee," Melvin said, forcing a smile.

Chad tossed the sodden clothes onto the porch and turned back to Melvin, glaring. "I should have left your butt down there and let you walk out."

"I'll be all right," Melvin said, and reached out to squeeze Chad's arm. "I wanna take a shower now. Have the coffee ready when I get out."

With an I-give-up gesture, Chad rushed inside the camp house and got the old man two towels, another pair of long johns and socks for his feet. He put them in the narrow bathroom and turned on the electric heater. Melvin leaned against the porch post and watched him.

In truth, except for the pain in his side, Melvin felt pretty good—better than he expected, considering. But in the back of his mind, he wondered if he might be in trouble.

A man like him never went to a doctor much. Martha didn't like that part of him, and they'd had a few words over the years about it. In fact, it had been six years since he'd even been to a doctor. And that was only when he was pretty sure he had influenza. No one who'd lived through the epidemic of 1918 messed around with *that*. So yes, maybe he *should* get to a doctor. But "maybe" was all he felt. It really didn't make any difference right now. The Flat Creek Bridge was flooded out.

No, he decided, *the soreness will probably heal itself and move on like a bad storm*.

He looked up. The stars looked so close and the air, though cold, was clear and clean. Fresh air was always appealing to him. That made him alive, cured him of most of what ailed him these sixty-eight years.

When Chad emerged from the bathroom, Melvin went inside, closed the door and latched it behind him. He looked in the mirror but wasn't shocked at what he saw, just bent forward to observe the gash, rotating his face from side to side. He attempted to wash the wound with soap and water by pressing and the gash started to bleed, dripping into the sink, so he stopped. He felt the lump with his hand and leaned back from the mirror, staring into his tired eyes.

I wonder what Martha would say if she saw me in this shape, he mused. *Glad she's not here to see me like this. She and Chad would be double-teaming me 'bout now.* In spite of the pain in his heart at remembering her, he smiled.

When he looked into the mirror, the intuition that he felt took a man's courage to accept. He needed strength now, and the thought of Mossback's courage gave him that. He would accept his wounds and go about his business like a man.

In the back of his mind, he knew one day his time would be up. But not now. He still had lots of things he wanted to get done around the farm. Lots of family and friends he wanted to see. He wanted to feel the wind on his face again. Wanted to see the swamps, wanted to feel the rich, dark topsoil in his hands wanted more days to watch a sunrise and sunset.

In the shower, he carefully avoided the wounds as he washed his body. Bending down to clean his legs with a washrag was painful, but he managed. He wasn't about to give up just 'cause he was old.

When Melvin turned the shower off, he heard Chad's trunk crank up, then roar down the lane on the way to the main farmhouse. Probably heading to get what Melvin never kept at the camp house—bandages and ointments.

"Damn," he muttered. "Wished I'd known . . . I'd have

told him to leave the water dripping." But it was just as well. It was a good house, built solid and sturdy, just like the camp house. It would stand long after Melvin, and probably Chad was gone.

Melvin dried himself, avoiding the worst of the bumps, pulled on his long johns and shuffled into the kitchen. He took his note pad off the refrigerator and spent a minute or so writing something down, then started to put the pad back when he pulled it back down, wrote more, and then finally placed it where he always had.

Minutes later, he heard Chad pulling his truck around back. The truck door slammed shut, and Chad bounced up the steps onto the porch.

Melvin had made two cups of coffee and was sitting on the bench at the kitchen table, sipping one of them when Chad rushed in with a brown paper sack.

"You look like you been in a fight or something," Chad said, pulling cotton, alcohol, salve and masking tape out of the bag. "What happened?"

Melvin didn't answer, just kept sipping the dark brew.

When Chad started wiping the wounds with cotton and alcohol, Melvin grimaced and swore a couple of times, but otherwise remained still.

"I'm gonna pull that cut closed," Chad said. "Then put some cotton and tape on it till we can get you to a doctor."

"I don't need a doctor for a cut." Melvin said. "Besides,

we can't get out now anyway. Better drink your coffee 'fore it gets cold."

"It's a nasty gash," Chad said, dismissing Melvin's attempt to change the subject. "Gonna need stitches, at the least. And your nose looks broke. What the hell happened?"

"Well . . . I saw a panther."

"A panther," Chad said. In his amazement, he stopped dabbing the cut above Melvin's eye and stepped back to look at him. "That must have been you shooting at it around dark. I was wondering who that was shooting. Figured it was you, but . . ."

Chad stopped speaking and looked away. He wanted to ask about the empty quiver, but couldn't bring himself to do it. *Not yet. Best to wait until Uncle Melvin brings it up himself. But . . .*

"Uncle Melvin," he said, "let me ask you something. . . . What were you doing in the flats wading around like that?"

"Oh, I wasn't wading around," Melvin replied, his tone careful. "I repaired the canoe and was floating out. I put in above the fallen log and floated out from there."

"Did the canoe flip on you or something?"

A pause, then, "You might say that."

After Chad finished doctoring Melvin the best way he could, he said, "I think I'm gonna go back down Fannie Road, see if the creek's still rising."

Exhausted from the hours of cold and lulled by the warmth from the propane stove, Melvin only nodded. The fight was finally out of him. If he could, he'd tell Chad about his adventure when he got back.

By the time he made it to the bunk and managed to zip up his sleeping bag, he heard Chad return and drive around the camp house. When Chad knocked on his open bedroom door, he was able to call out, "Come on in."

"Uncle Melvin, you asleep?"

"No, I'm just resting, thinking," Melvin said. "About where to go hunting tomorrow."

Chad leaned his head back, then lowered it to meet Melvin's eyes. "Uncle Melvin, there won't *be* any hunting tomorrow. We gotta get you to a doctor. The water's only a little higher than it was a while ago. You think the water will peak tonight and be down low enough to cross over the bridge tomorrow?"

Melvin nodded. "Yep, it'll be low enough. Probably 'bout ten in the morning if not sooner. Now let me ask *you* something. I'd like for you to make sure we get those fields back like they were."

"I promise," Chad said. "But let's talk about it in the morning—after we get you to the doctor."

"All right then … Chad?"

"Yes, sir?"

"That panther was goddamn beautiful."

Chad smiled. "Bet it was. I want to hear all about it—*tomorrow*. You look beat."

Melvin nodded, then looked at Chad in silence a moment before his eyes would no longer stay open. Chad got up, left the bedroom, and pulled the door closed.

* * *

The sensation was like the one you'd get upon hearing a sudden and unexpected sound. A feeling you'd get about traveling some place that has a bad reputation, some place you really don't want to go to. It turned around and around in his head, like it was spinning in a fast-moving current. He couldn't think coherently about it, but it meant nothing now. He attempted to lift his head, but his neck was sore and it took too much energy.

After a few moments, he got a sudden rush and sense of well-being, but still felt peeved for capsizing the canoe. It was such a stupid thing to do, and he knew it. He nearly swore when he thought about it.

Melvin heard the kitchen door close with a thump, and opened his eyes.

Chad must have decided to walk down the lane and get my truck. Melvin had told him the keys were on the floorboard. Melvin smiled. *Chad, you're a good man. Just like I knew you'd be.*

Melvin listened to Chad leave, closed his eyes and saw gray and black spots. The spots became images of the big buck and the panther. He felt the cold, and curled up in his sleeping bag.

After thirty minutes, near sleep, he heard Chad drive his truck around to the shed, park it, get out, and slam the truck door shut. A moment later, Chad's footsteps entered the kitchen.

Melvin heard the door to his room ease open for a moment, then click shut. He lay with his eyes closed, just listening, not thinking; nothing stirred in his thoughts. Another twenty minutes went by before he heard Chad go into his bedroom and close the door.

* * *

Melvin was in deep sleep when he woke up. He felt down along his side, pressed the swollen spot, and heard a low burst of static in his skin. It was hard to breathe now, but the pain in his stomach was subsiding, at least.

If I can just make it to daylight. Daylight was when he became young again, unbeatable.

He looked out the window and saw stars buried in the sky. Closed his eyes and in his mind's eye was a huge oak tree. He lay warm and comfortable, content, listening to the sounds of the swamps, inviting him in. He heard the owls hoot, then the coyotes yelping in the distance, and he was pleased. He felt his breathing slow.

In a dark realm, he started drifting, dreaming. Dreaming he was an Indian with a dog, stalking a big black panther with his longbow in a forest of enormous cypress trees laden in silk, a place where diamonds dangled from the leathery green leaves of enormous oaks. There was no sun, just a sky of yellow gold. He was happy and unafraid.

On the wall in the kitchen where the bow quiver hung, the hawk's tail feather rose, then rocked as it slowly drifted down.

The End

* * *

About the Author

Mossback came about over the course of ten years, in which author Kenneth Fore mentally struggled for an ending that was both uplifting, and realistic. When he found it, he began writing Mossback. Mossback is based on a true story. This is the second edition of Mossback.

A writer for many years, Kenneth Fore's published works can be found in several venues and he is also an award winning writer with the short story Sweetness in the Hunt. *MOSSBACK* was Ken's first full-length novel, and THE WOLF TATTOO his second novel. His third novel ORION will be out in 2014. You can join Ken on Facebook and Twitter. Webpage is Kennethfore.com